HEAT SEEKER
COMBUSTION
A GUN HONEY SERIES

HARD CASE CRIME

TITAN COMICS

HEAT SEEKER
COMBUSTION
A GUN HONEY SERIES

GROUP EDITOR Jake Devine	**HEAD OF PRODUCTION** Kevin Wooff	**SALES & CIRCULATION MANAGER** Steve Tothill
DESIGNER Dan Bura	**PRODUCTION MANAGER** Jackie Flook	**HEAD OF RIGHTS** Rosanna Anness
SENIOR CREATIVE EDITOR David Manley-Leach	**PRODUCTION CONTROLLERS** Caterina Falqui & Kelly Fenlon	**RIGHTS EXECUTIVE** Pauline Savouré
EDITOR Jonathan Wilkins	**PUBLICITY MANAGER** Will O'Mullane	**HEAD OF CREATIVE & BUSINESS DEVELOPMENT** Duncan Baizley
ASSISTANT EDITOR Ibraheem Kazi	**PUBLICIST** Caitlin Storer	**PUBLISHING DIRECTORS** Ricky Claydon & John Dziewiatkowski
EDITORIAL ASSISTANT Holly Smith	**DIRECT MARKET SALES COORDINATOR** Chief Stride	**CHIEF OPERATING OFFICER** Andrew Sumner
ART DIRECTOR Oz Browne	**DIGITAL & MARKETING MANAGER** Jo Teather	**PUBLISHERS** Vivian Cheung & Nick Landau
DESIGNERS David Colderley & Matt Bookman	**MARKETING COORDINATOR** Lauren Noding	

HEAT SEEKER: COMBUSTION: A GUN HONEY SERIES, VOLUME TWO

STANDARD EDITION ISBN: 9781787743304
DIRECT MARKET EDITION ISBN: 9781787744899
DIRECT MARKET EDITION ISBN: 9781787744905

Published by Titan Comics, a division of Titan Publishing Group, Ltd.,
144 Southwark Street, London SE1 OUP, UK.

© Winterfall LLC, 2025. The name 'Hard Case Crime' and the Hard Case Crime logo are trademarks of Winterfall LLC. Hard Case Crime comics are produced with editorial guidance by Charles Ardai. All Rights Reserved. No portion of this book may be reproduced or transmitted in any form or by any means, without the express permission of the publisher, Titan Comics.

EU RP eucomply OÜ Pärnu mnt 139b-14 11317 Tallinn, Estonia hello@eucompliancepartner.com +3375690241

A CIP catalogue record for this title is available from the British Library

10 9 8 7 6 5 4 3 2 1

First Published July 2025

Printed in Spain

WWW.TITAN-COMICS.COM

BECOME A FAN ON FACEBOOK.COM/COMICSTITAN   **FOLLOW US ON TWITTER @COMICSTITAN**

For rights information contact Rosanna.anness@titanemail.com

HEAT SEEKER
COMBUSTION
A GUN HONEY SERIES

WRITER
CHARLES ARDAI

PENCILLER
ACE CONTINUADO

INKER
JUAN CASTRO

COLORIST
ASIFUR RAHMAN

LETTERER
DAVID LEACH

CHAPTER ONE

Illustrated by:
David Nakayama

"YOU'VE GOT TO GET MY DAUGHTER OUT OF HERE, MS. RACERS.

"IT'S NOT SAFE. THEY'LL TRY TO USE HER TO COERCE ME."

WHERE'S FATHER?

"SHE NEEDS TO DISAPPEAR."

...AND YOU?

OH, THEY WON'T DO ANYTHING TO *ME*. THEY CAN'T. I'M THEIR GOLDEN GOOSE.

THEY JUST WANT TO FORCE ME TO KEEP LAYING.

The Biochemistry Revolution by Dr. Bessemer Preiss

WHERE AM I SUPPOSED TO TAKE HER? A 12-YEAR-OLD CAN'T HIDE OUT ON HER OWN.

MONTEFIACCO. THE NUNS WILL KNOW WHAT TO DO.

BUT FIRST--

"--FIRST YOU'LL NEED TO GET HER OUT OF VENICE."
QUICK-- INTO THE BOAT.
BLAM!
BLAM!
DON'T HIT THE GIRL!

GET UNDER THE BENCH AND DON'T MOVE.
YOU READY?
NOW SHE ASKS ME.
GO AFTER THEM! NOW!
WHAMM

URRK--
URRM!
RIGHT ON SCHEDULE.
YOU DIDN'T KILL THEM, DID YOU?
NOT IF THEY KNOW HOW TO SWIM.
GOOD. THE TRAIL CESAR LAID SHOULD KEEP THEM SPINNING THEIR WHEELS.

Panel 1:
IF YOU DON'T NEED ME, THEN--

Panel 2:
WHERE'S FATHER.

FATHER WILL KNOW WHAT TO DO. HE ALWAYS KNOWS WHAT TO DO.

Panel 3:
YOUR FATHER *HIRED* ME, TO PROTECT YOU. TO HELP YOU.

...THEN HELP ME GO HOME.

Panel 4:
HOME'S NOT SAFE, NOT NOW.

WHEN IT IS, I'LL TAKE YOU BACK. BUT RIGHT NOW YOU HAVE TO TRUST ME. LIKE YOUR FATHER HAS.

Panel 5:
SHE'S GOOD WITH KIDS, HUH?

GET IN LINE.

MONTEFIACCO, ITALY.

NORMAL PEOPLE COME TO THE DOLOMITES TO SKI, TO DRINK WINE, SIT IN A SAUNA.

NOT TO ESCAPE TRIGGER-HAPPY GUNMEN WHILE TRYING TO DELIVER A PACKAGE THAT WISHES SHE'D NEVER BEEN MAILED.

BUT THIS IS WHAT I DO.

EVEN IN THE DEAD OF WINTER, I DRAW THE HEAT.

IS THAT A CASTLE?

A CONVENT.

NUNS? THEY'RE GOING TO MAKE ME *PRAY* ALL THE TIME!

YOU CAN PRAY THAT THEY WON'T.

DO WE KNOCK OR JUST WALK IN?

ACCORDING TO THE PROFESSOR--

--THEY'LL BE EXPECTING YOU.
I'VE SENT THEM DONATIONS OVER THE YEARS. *TITHES*, FROM MY INVENTIONS.
THEY CAN DO THIS ONE THING FOR ME.
SOME WOULD SAY TITHING IS A SIGN OF A GUILTY CONSCIENCE, DOCTOR.
WHAT EXACTLY ***ARE*** THESE INVENTIONS OF YOURS? AND WHO BUYS THEM FROM YOU?
YOU MIGHT THINK YOU WOULD BE HAPPIER KNOWING MORE, BUT IT ISN'T SO.
The Biochemistry Revolution by Bessemer
TAKE THE BOOK. WHAT I CAN SAY ABOUT MY WORK IS IN THERE.
AND PLEASE-- ***PLEASE***-- TAKE CARE.

SHOULD'VE KNOCKED.
LITTLE COLD TO BE PLAYING LADY GODIVA, ISN'T IT?
IS IT?
THEY SAID THERE'D BE NO TOUR GROUPS TODAY.
WHAT SORT OF CONVENT *IS* THIS?
NOT OUR LADY OF THE IMMACULATE SADDLE, I CAN TELL YOU THAT.
MISS RACERS? YOU'RE A BIT EARLY, AREN'T YOU. OH MY.
WELL, THE PHOTOGRAPHY WILL BE OVER SOON. BROCHURE FOR ONE OF THE HEALTH SPAS UP THE MOUNTAIN. A BIT ***NAKED***, I KNOW, BUT THEY PAY A FEE TO SHOOT HERE AND IT HELPS US FEED THE HUNGRY, DOESN'T IT.
MAY I SHOW YOU TO YOUR ROOMS?

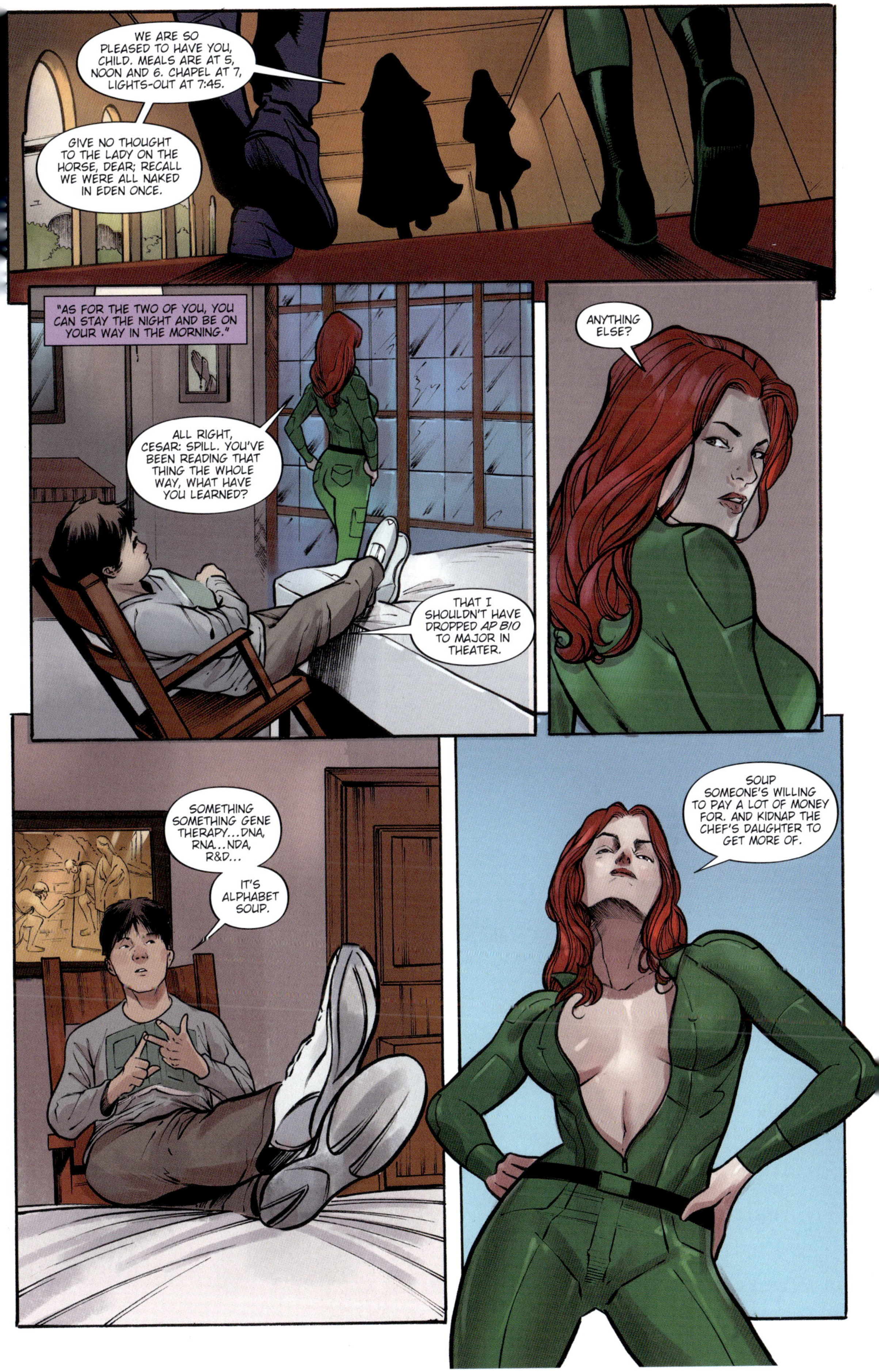
WE ARE SO PLEASED TO HAVE YOU, CHILD. MEALS ARE AT 5, NOON AND 6. CHAPEL AT 7, LIGHTS-OUT AT 7:45.
GIVE NO THOUGHT TO THE LADY ON THE HORSE, DEAR; RECALL WE WERE ALL NAKED IN EDEN ONCE.
"AS FOR THE TWO OF YOU, YOU CAN STAY THE NIGHT AND BE ON YOUR WAY IN THE MORNING."
ALL RIGHT, CESAR: SPILL. YOU'VE BEEN READING THAT THING THE WHOLE WAY, WHAT HAVE YOU LEARNED?
THAT I SHOULDN'T HAVE DROPPED *AP BIO* TO MAJOR IN THEATER.
ANYTHING ELSE?
SOMETHING SOMETHING GENE THERAPY...DNA, RNA...NDA, R&D...
IT'S ALPHABET SOUP.
SOUP SOMEONE'S WILLING TO PAY A LOT OF MONEY FOR. AND KIDNAP THE CHEF'S DAUGHTER TO GET MORE OF.

HE SAYS HIS TECHNIQUES COULD 'ENHANCE HUMAN RESISTANCE.'
RESISTANCE? TO WHAT?
ALL SORTS OF THINGS--DISEASE, FATIGUE, HUNGER, HEAT, COLD...
LITTLE COLD TO BE PLAYING LADY GODIVA, ISN'T IT?
IS IT?
SHIT.
IT'S IMPOSSIBLE! THEY COULDN'T HAVE FOLLOWED US!
THEY *DIDN'T*. SOMEHOW THEY GOT HERE *FIRST*.
IT'S ALMOST LIGHTS-OUT.
PRAY WE'RE NOT TOO LATE.

"SHE'S JUST A KID, MARCO."

"WE'VE GOT ORDERS."

"MARCO!"

"WHAT THE--?"

CRASH!

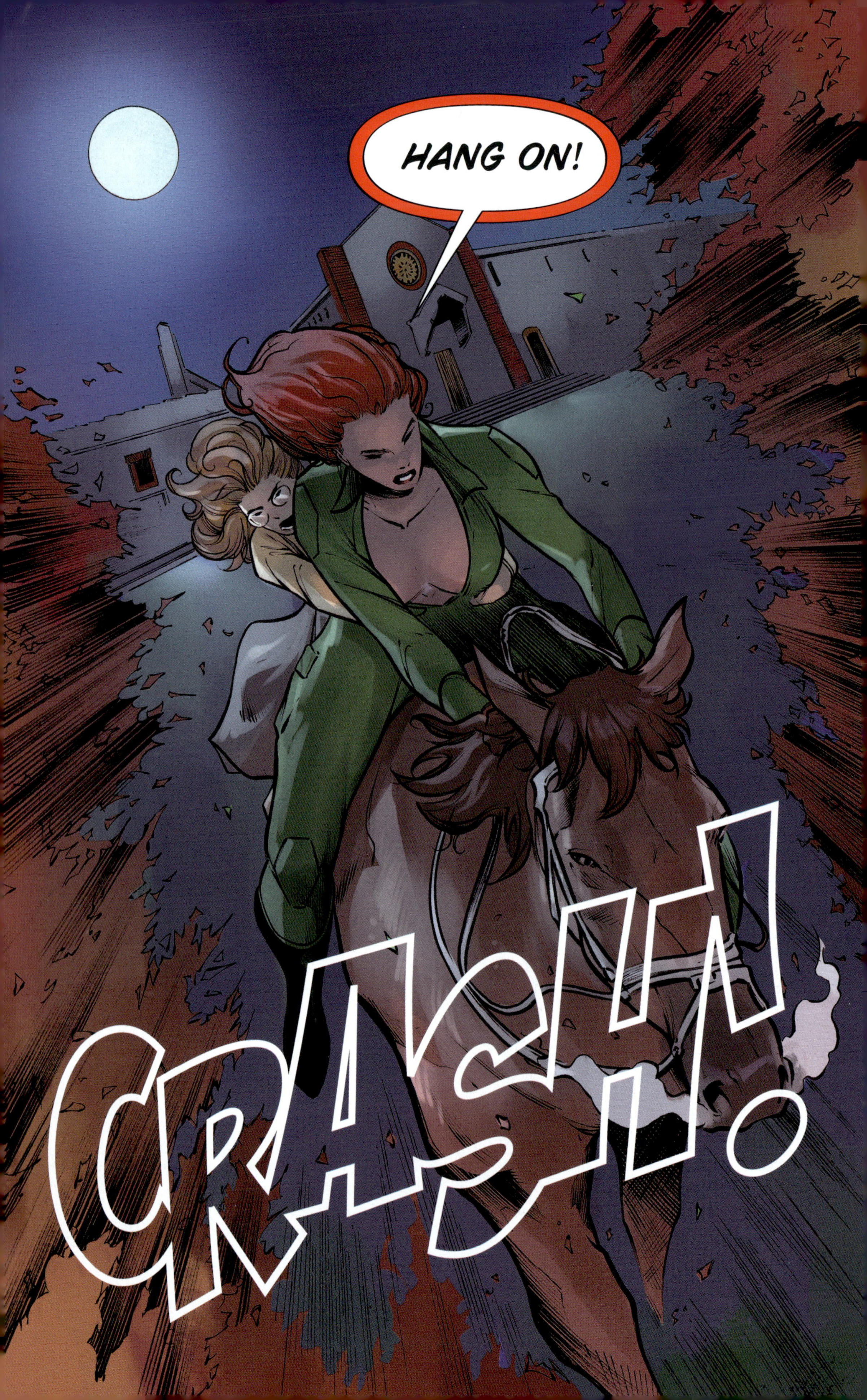
HANG ON!
CRASH!

BLAM!
SMASH!
HOW THE HELL DO WE FOLLOW HER...? SHE'S ON HORSEBACK... UP THE MOUNTAIN... THE CAR CAN'T--
DRIVE UP THROUGH BRACCO. I'LL GO ON FOOT.
YOU'RE BLEEDING.
JUST A FLESH WOUND. GET MOVING.
I'VE GOT SOME QUESTIONS FOR YOU.
OH, DEAR, I COULDN'T--
JUST THINK OF IT AS CONFESSION.

THIS MUST BE WHERE THEY WERE SHOOTING THE BROCHURE FOR--
THERE'S NO BROCHURE. IT WAS A ***LIE***.
Quietus
SPA
SAUNA
IT'S A FUNNY THING ABOUT LIES. I LIE FOR A LIVING. I'M A ***CONNOISSEUR*** OF LIES.
BUT THAT DOESN'T MAKE IT FEEL ANY BETTER WHEN SOMEONE LIES TO ME.
LET'S GO AROUND THE OTHER WAY.
YOU KNOW FATHER'S GERMAN, RIGHT? HE TOOK ME TO BADEN-BADEN WHEN I WAS NINE.
GOOD FOR HIM. WE'RE GOING THE OTHER WAY.
YOU CAN STAY HERE TILL MORNING. I'LL FIND US A WAY OFF THE MOUNTAIN.
INFERMERIA
ERSTE HILFE

"STAY AWAY FROM THE WINDOWS AND KEEP THE LIGHTS *OFF*."

GET IN. NOW!

WHO ELSE KNEW? WHO KNEW ABOUT THE KID?

WE ALL KNEW! THAT SHE WAS COMING, I MEAN. ONLY I KNEW WHOSE DAUGHTER SHE WAS.
THEN HOW DID THOSE TWO KNOW TO COME HERE?
SOMEONE MUST HAVE TIPPED THEM OFF.
WOULD YOU PLEASE PUT THAT INSTRUMENT OF VIOLENCE AWAY, YOUNG MAN? THIS IS A HOUSE OF GOD.
IT'S A HOUSE OF VIOLENCE TONIGHT, SISTER.
FATHER...?
ROSALINE? YOU KNOW BETTER THAN TO CALL--IT COULD BE TRACED--
PEOPLE WERE WAITING FOR US AT THE CONVENT, FATHER. WHO WERE THEY?
I...I DON'T KNOW.
RATTLE-- RATTLE--
I'VE GOT TO GO.
SMASH!

WOULD YOU PLEASE COME OUT AND HELP?
I WOULDN'T HAVE BROKEN IN IF I'D KNOWN SOMEONE WAS STILL HERE. I JUST... I'VE LOST A LOT OF BLOOD. COULD USE A HAND.
WELL HOLY SHIT.
YOU'RE A KID.
DO YOU WANT HELP OR NOT?
I CAN HANDLE ONE OF THOSE. FATHER TAUGHT ME. HE'S A DOCTOR.
WHY WOULD YOU HELP ME?
YOU ASKED ME TO.
SAID YOU'D LOST A LOT OF BLOOD.
CLK-- CLK-- CLK--
YOU'RE ONE OF FATHER'S, AREN'T YOU? I STAPLED YOUR ARM AND YOU DIDN'T EVEN SAY OW.
HE'D WANT ME TO HELP.
WAIT, PREISS IS YOUR FATHER? JESUS CHRIST.
GUESS I'M DAVID PROWSE AND THEY DIDN'T TRUST ME WITH THE SCRIPT.

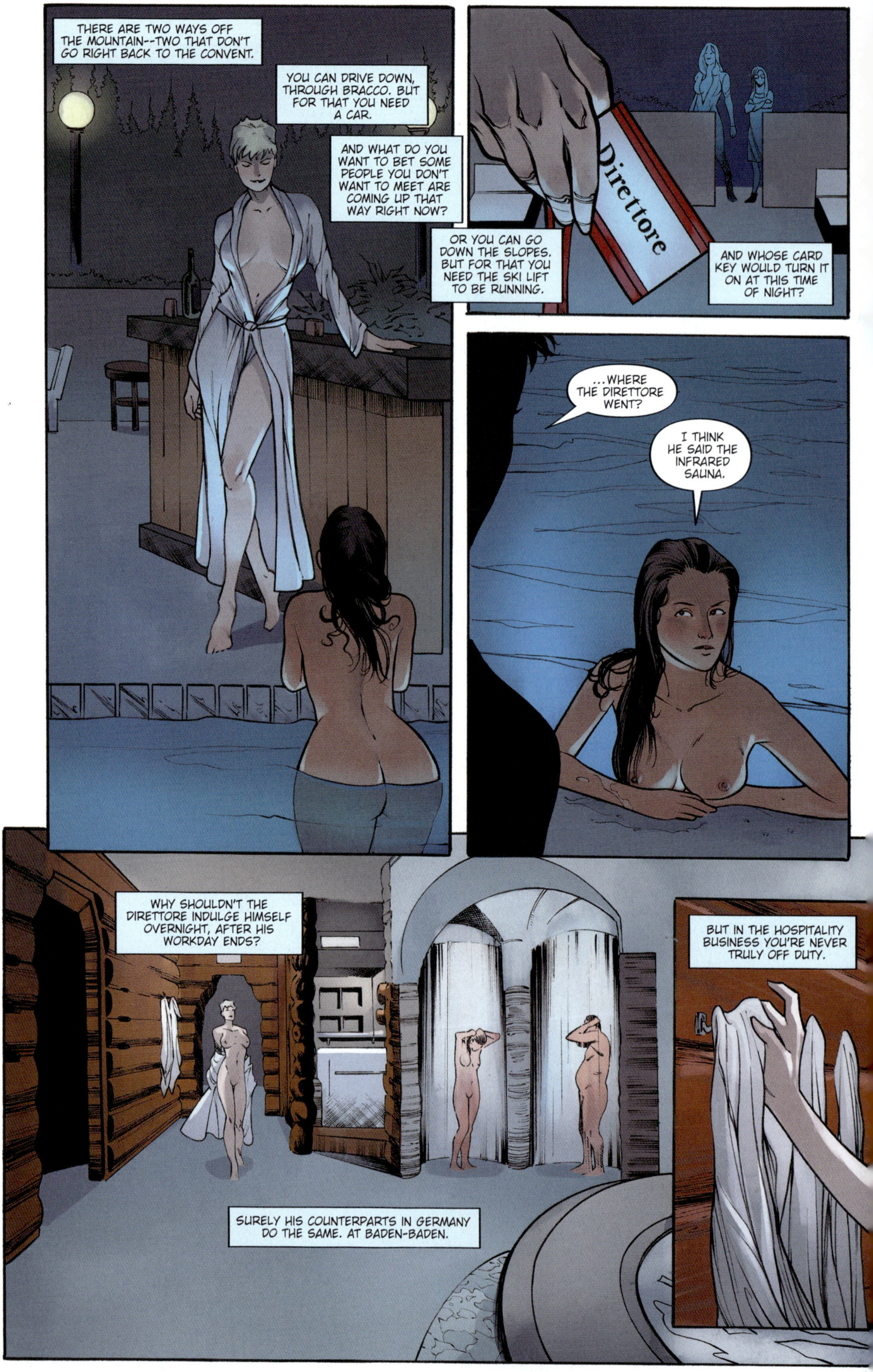
THERE ARE TWO WAYS OFF THE MOUNTAIN--TWO THAT DON'T GO RIGHT BACK TO THE CONVENT.
YOU CAN DRIVE DOWN, THROUGH BRACCO. BUT FOR THAT YOU NEED A CAR.
AND WHAT DO YOU WANT TO BET SOME PEOPLE YOU DON'T WANT TO MEET ARE COMING UP THAT WAY RIGHT NOW?
OR YOU CAN GO DOWN THE SLOPES. BUT FOR THAT YOU NEED THE SKI LIFT TO BE RUNNING.
Direttore
AND WHOSE CARD KEY WOULD TURN IT ON AT THIS TIME OF NIGHT?
...WHERE THE DIRETTORE WENT?
I THINK HE SAID THE INFRARED SAUNA.
WHY SHOULDN'T THE DIRETTORE INDULGE HIMSELF OVERNIGHT, AFTER HIS WORKDAY ENDS?
SURELY HIS COUNTERPARTS IN GERMANY DO THE SAME. AT BADEN-BADEN.
BUT IN THE HOSPITALITY BUSINESS YOU'RE NEVER TRULY OFF DUTY.

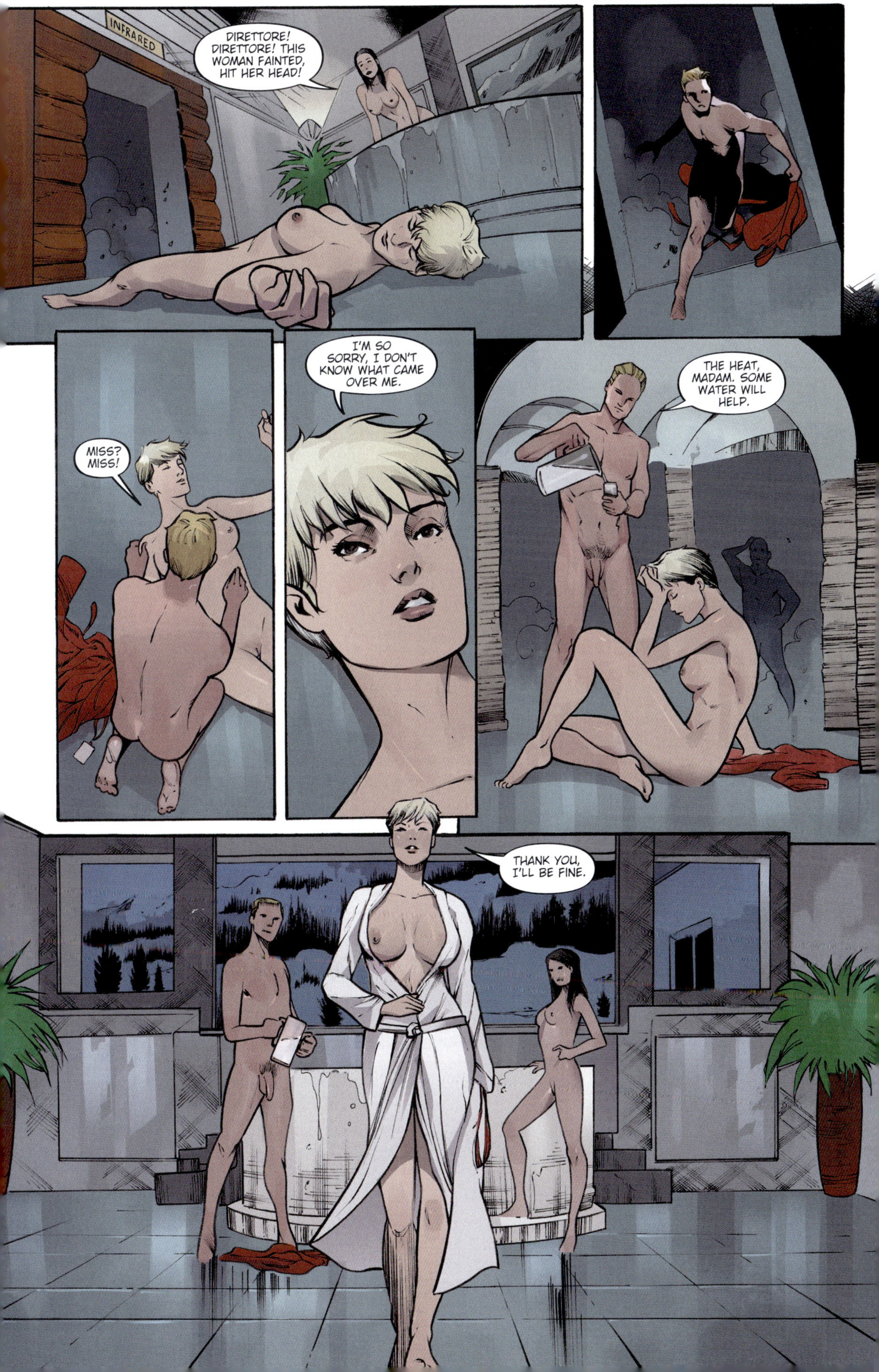
INFRARED
DIRETTORE! DIRETTORE! THIS WOMAN FAINTED, HIT HER HEAD!
MISS? MISS!
I'M SO SORRY, I DON'T KNOW WHAT CAME OVER ME.
THE HEAT, MADAM. SOME WATER WILL HELP.
THANK YOU, I'LL BE FINE.

STEP 1-- GET THE LIFT RUNNING.

STEP 2--

SHIT.

CRRRNCH!

CRRRNCH!

SEARCH EVERYWHERE! I'LL MEET YOU AT THE SUMMIT.

WHERE WOULD I GO IF I WERE A FRIGHTENED 12-YEAR-OLD?

WHERE WOULD NO ONE LOOK FOR ME...?
GET OUT OF HERE, KID. I'M NOT TAKING YOU IN.
FIND SOME BETTER PLACE TO HIDE.
ALL BY YOURSELF, HUH?
THAT'S A GOOD GIRL.
YOUR UNCLE MARCO'S GONNA TAKE YOU WHERE YOU NEED TO BE.
I'M NOT GOING ANYWHERE WITH YOU!
TRY TO RUN, I'LL SHOOT YOU IN THE KNEES.
WE NEED YOU ALIVE. WE DON'T NEED YOU ABLE TO WALK.
BLAM!

MS. RACERS! YOU FOUND ME!
IN THE IMMORTAL WORDS OF ARNOLD SCHWARZENEGGER--
COME WITH ME IF YOU WANT TO LIVE.

Model: Grace McClung

CHAPTER TWO

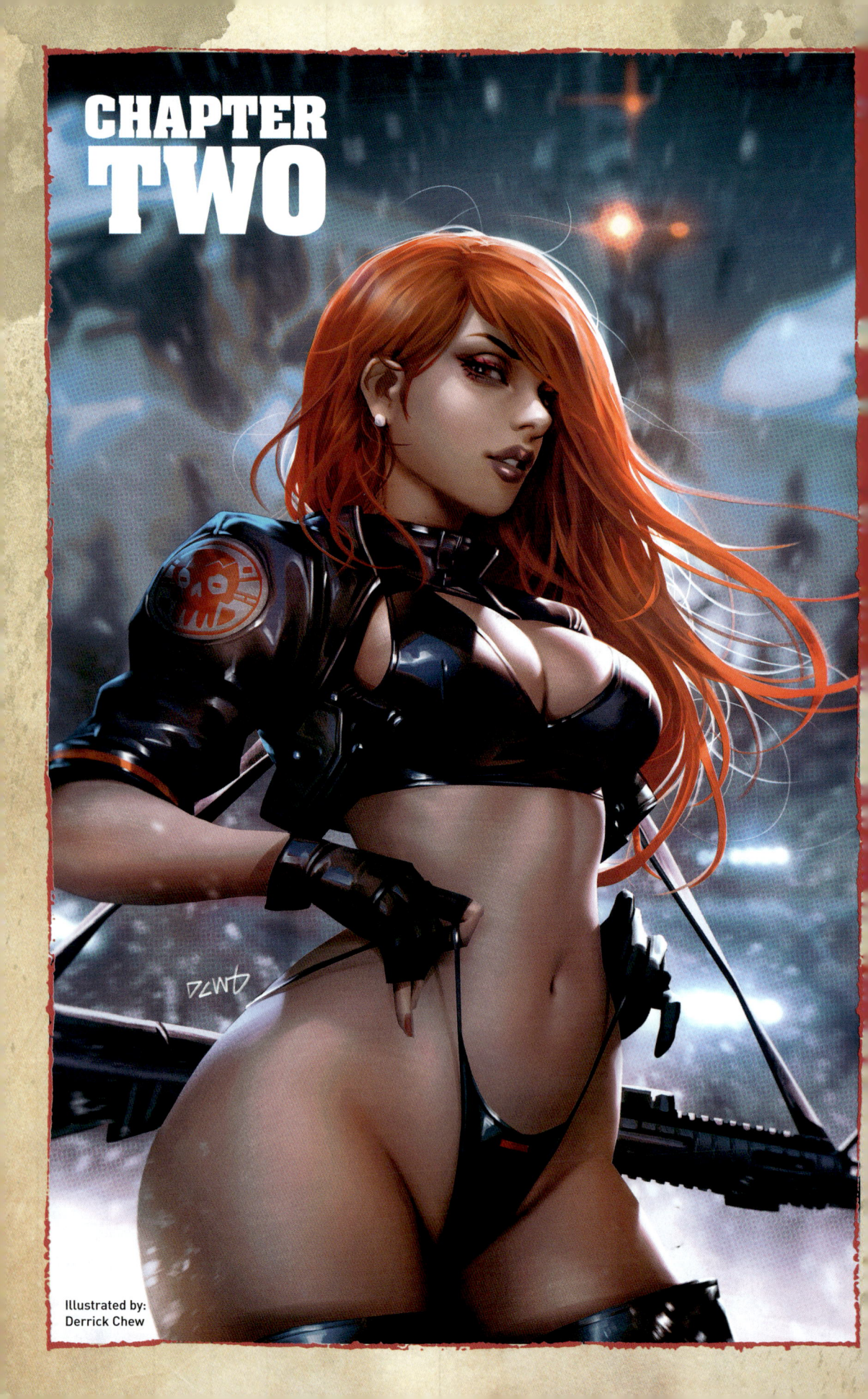

Illustrated by: Derrick Chew

I HELP PEOPLE DISAPPEAR.
IT'S WHAT I DO.
I'M GOOD AT IT--MAYBE THE BEST THERE IS.
I'M NOT USED TO PEOPLE DISAPPEARING ON ME.
ESPECIALLY NOT A 12-YEAR-OLD GIRL.
ONE WHOSE FATHER HIRED ME TO DELIVER HER TO A MOUNTAIN SANCTUARY.
BUT HERE WE ARE.
THE QUESTION IS, WHERE IS SHE--
BLAM!
OH HELL.

I DON'T KNOW IF ROSALINE PREISS IS ALIVE OR DEAD RIGHT NOW.

BUT IF SHE'S ALIVE, HER BEST CHANCE OF STAYING THAT WAY IS IF I GET TO HER FIRST.

SKNNNG! SKNNNG!

I CAN SIT AND WAIT UNTIL WE ALL REACH THE TOP TOGETHER. OR I CAN BET ON NEITHER OF THOSE MEN HAVING PUT IN 11 YEARS ON BALANCE BEAM.

OF COURSE, A BALANCE BEAM'S NOT A NARROW METAL CABLE SWAYING IN THE ALPINE WINDS.

BUT THAT'S WHAT THE SUMMER WITH THE WALLENDAS WAS FOR.

BLAM! BLAM!
SILVER LINING: THE SWAYING AND THE WIND AREN'T DOING THEIR AIM ANY FAVORS.
SPANNNG!
FOCUS, DAHLIA. FOCUS.
ANOTHER SLIP LIKE THAT ONE, AND ROSALINE PREISS WILL NEED SOMEONE ELSE TO RESCUE HER.

Panel 1:
— COME ON, KID. WE'VE GOT TO GET MOVING.
— YOU *KILLED* HIM!

Panel 2:
— WHO KNOWS? MAYBE HE HAD A HEART ATTACK THE INSTANT BEFORE THE BULLET WENT IN.

Panel 3:
— BUT... WHY WOULD YOU DO THAT TO HELP *ME*?
— YOU HELPED ME. BESIDES. YOU EVER HEAR "WITH GREAT POWER COMES GREAT RESPONSIBILITY"?

Panel 4:
— ISN'T THAT SPIDER-MAN?
— SURE IS. A PERSON'S GOT TO DRAW THE LINE SOMEWHERE. YOU DON'T DESERVE WHAT'S BEEN DONE TO YOU. BY YOUR OWN FATHER.

Panel 5:
— HE JUST SENT ME AWAY SO I'D BE SOMEWHERE SAFE! HE DIDN'T KNOW... *THIS* WOULD HAPPEN!
— GET ON. WE'LL TALK ABOUT IT LATER.

ONE GUNSHOT. ONE BODY.
SO SHE'S ALIVE.
FOR NOW.
AND SINCE I DON'T REMEMBER HANDING THE 12-YEAR-OLD A GUN, I'M GUESSING LADY GODIVA AND HER PHOTOGRAPHER OVER THERE HAD A FALLING OUT.
JUST AS WELL.
THAT'S ONE DOWN. THREE TO GO.
...AND THAT'S ROSALINE, IN BACK. PROBABLY TOO SCARED TO ROLL OFF INTO THE SNOW AT THAT SPEED. PLUS MAYBE SHE REALIZES MORE BAD GUYS ARE--
--CLOSE BEHIND.

BLAM!
BLAINE WANTED ME TO DESIGN A SKIING ILLUSION FOR HIM ONCE. I TURNED HIM DOWN.
BLAM!
TOO DIFFICULT, TOO DANGEROUS TO PERFORM.
BUT THAT DOESN'T MEAN I DIDN'T KNOW HOW I WOULD'VE DONE IT.
BLAM!
BLAM!
BLAM!
HE WANTED TO DISAPPEAR IN MOTION-- SKI OFF THE SIDE OF A CLIFF AND JUST...VANISH. WHILE A CAMERA FILMED CONTINUOUSLY.
CLK
CLK
IT CAN BE DONE. BUT THE TIMING'S A KILLER.

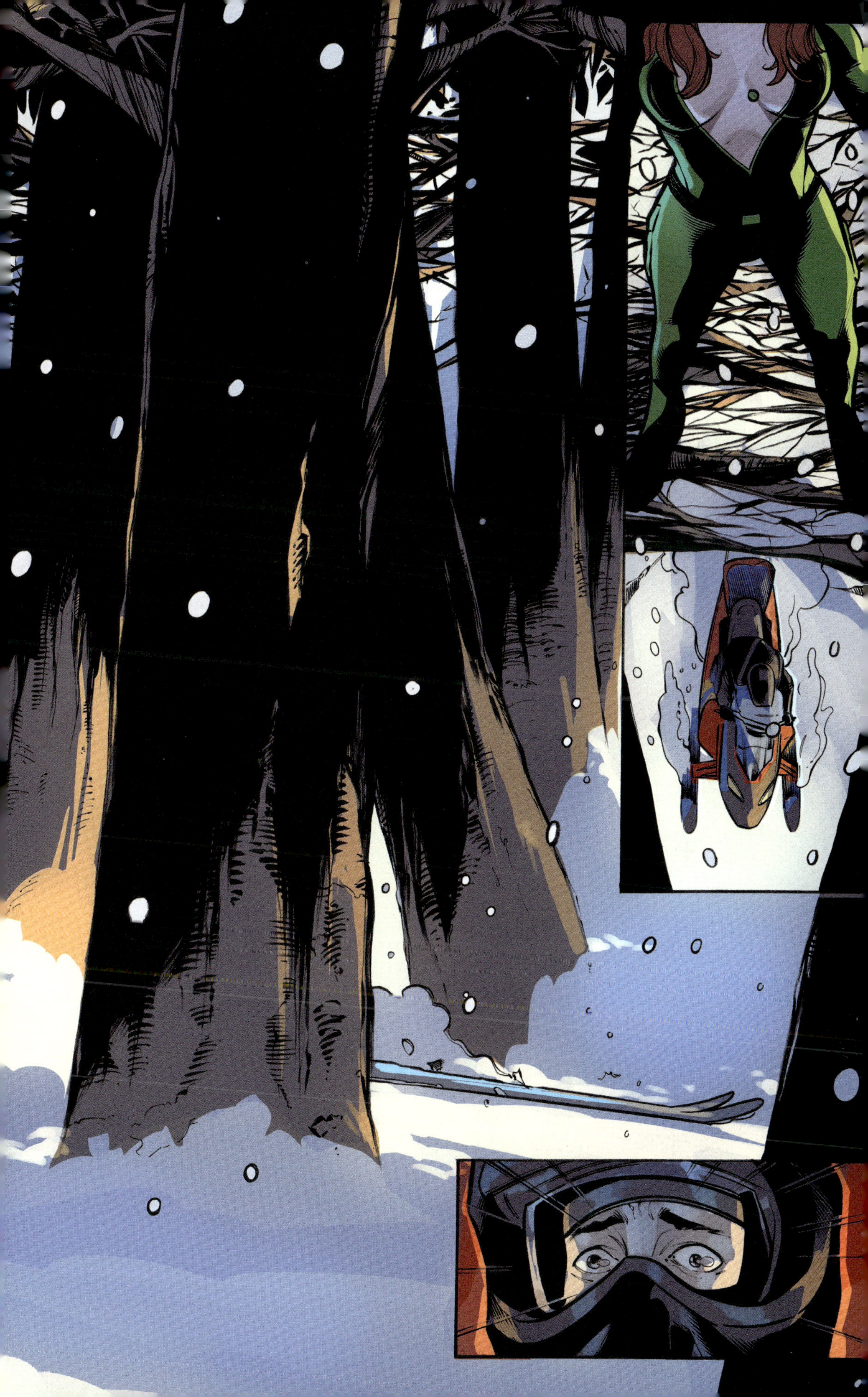

AAAAHHGGH!

AND THEN THERE WERE TWO.

EVERY MINUTE THIS GOES ON IS A MINUTE ROSALINE GETS FARTHER AWAY.

SO IT'S TIME TO END IT.

HELLO, HANDSOME.

YES, YOU. YOU'RE A VERY HANDSOME MAN.

AND THAT'S WHAT THE SUMMER WITH DARCI LYNNE WAS FOR.

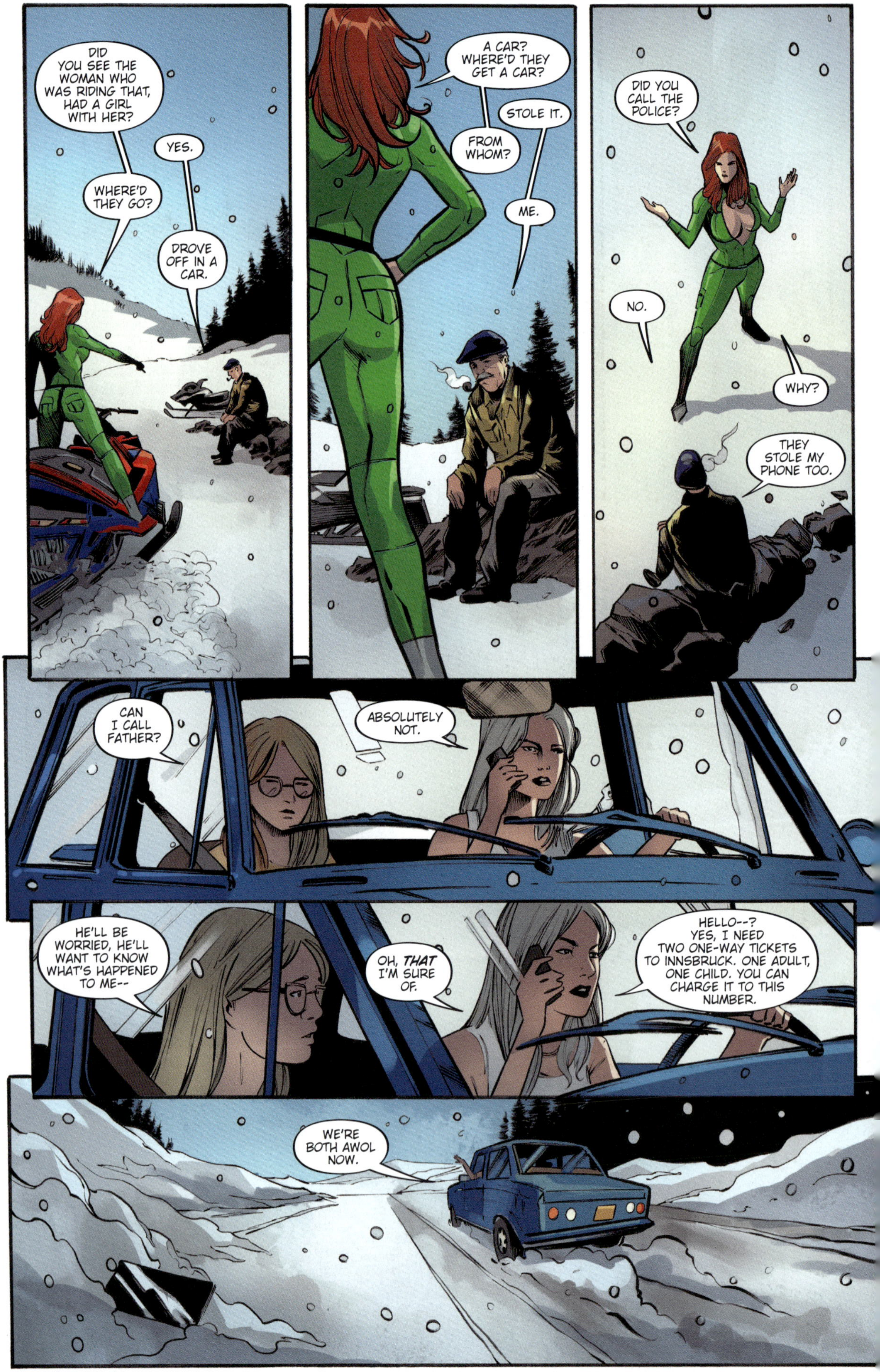

DID YOU SEE THE WOMAN WHO WAS RIDING THAT, HAD A GIRL WITH HER?
YES.
WHERE'D THEY GO?
DROVE OFF IN A CAR.
A CAR? WHERE'D THEY GET A CAR?
STOLE IT.
FROM WHOM?
ME.
DID YOU CALL THE POLICE?
NO.
WHY?
THEY STOLE MY PHONE TOO.
CAN I CALL FATHER?
ABSOLUTELY NOT.
HE'LL BE WORRIED, HE'LL WANT TO KNOW WHAT'S HAPPENED TO ME--
OH, *THAT* I'M SURE OF.
HELLO--? YES, I NEED TWO ONE-WAY TICKETS TO INNSBRUCK. ONE ADULT, ONE CHILD. YOU CAN CHARGE IT TO THIS NUMBER.
WE'RE BOTH AWOL NOW.

I DON'T THINK YOU'RE GOING TO CALL THEM EITHER.
WHY'S THAT?
I *MIGHT* OVERLOOK YOUR KILLING THREE OF MY MEN, IF YOU GIVE US THE GIRL.
I'M LOOKING FOR HER THE SAME AS YOU ARE.
IF THAT'S SO, IT'S MOST UNFORTUNATE FOR YOU. IT MEANS YOU HAVE NOTHING TO OFFER.
SNAP--
FIRE AT WILL.
NO!

STOP THIS IMMEDIATELY! HOW DARE YOU VIOLATE THE HOLY RIGHT OF SANCTUARY?
THIS WOMAN--
AND THIS MAN.
AND THIS MAN! ARE BOTH UNDER THE SWORN PROTECTION OF THE SISTERS OF MONTEFIACCO!
'SISTERS'? I ONLY SEE ONE OF YOU, AND WITH ALL DUE RESPECT, THERE ARE SEVEN OF US.
STEP ASIDE.
THEY'RE JUST A BIT SLOWER-- ARTHRITIS, DON'T YOU KNOW.
BUT THEY'RE HERE NOW, AND SISTER MARGARITA IS FILMING EVERYTHING, SO UNLESS YOU WANT YOUR MURDER OF TWO INNOCENTS TO BE WATCHED BY MILLIONS OF AMERICANS ON THEIR "YOUTUBE," I SUGGEST YOU DESIST NOW.
THIS ISN'T OVER.

SISTER MARGARITA?
HOW'D YOU FIND ME?
JUST FOLLOWED THE GUNSHOTS AND THE SCREAMING.
TAKE OVER DRIVING, CESAR. YOU LOSE OUR TAIL AND I'LL GET OUR DESTINATION.
YOU'RE GOING TO HELP US TRACE YOUR PHONE. NO PROMISES ABOUT THE CAR.
WE NEED TO KNOW WHAT CALLS THEY MADE, AND ANY TRANSACTIONS.
Innsbruck

INNSBRUCK, AUSTRIA
WHY ARE WE HERE?
I GREW UP HERE. ALL MY STUFF IS HERE.
THEN WON'T THEY LOOK FOR YOU HERE?
THAT'S WHY WE'RE NOT STAYING LONG.
WHERE ARE WE HEADING AFTER THIS?
DO YOU EVER STOP ASKING QUESTIONS?
'CAUSE I WAS PICTURING MORE OF A BABY YODA SORT OF THING, WHERE YOU TAG ALONG, LOOK CUTE, AND DON'T TALK MUCH.
ARE WE GOING TO EAT SOON? I'M HUNGRY.
I'VE GOT SOME MREs IN HERE SOMEWHERE. IF YOU FIND 'EM, YOU CAN EAT 'EM.
WOW. YOU MUST REALLY LOVE COMIC BOOKS.
LOT OF THESE WERE MY DAD'S. BUT YEAH. THEY GOT ME THROUGH SOME TOUGH TIMES.

READ ANY OF THEM YOU WANT WHILE I PULL SOME STUFF TOGETHER.
WE'RE GONNA NEED LIGHTSABERS WHERE WE'RE GOING?
HOKEY RELIGIONS AND ANCIENT WEAPONS ARE NO MATCH FOR A GOOD BLASTER AT YOUR SIDE, KID.
WIPE YOURSELF DOWN. NO TELLING HOW LONG BEFORE WE GET ANOTHER CHANCE.
THERE'S A SACHET OF WATER, YOU SQUEEZE IT ON THE SPONGE, THEN DRY WITH THE TOWEL.
SHOUT WHEN YOU'RE DONE.
SAF

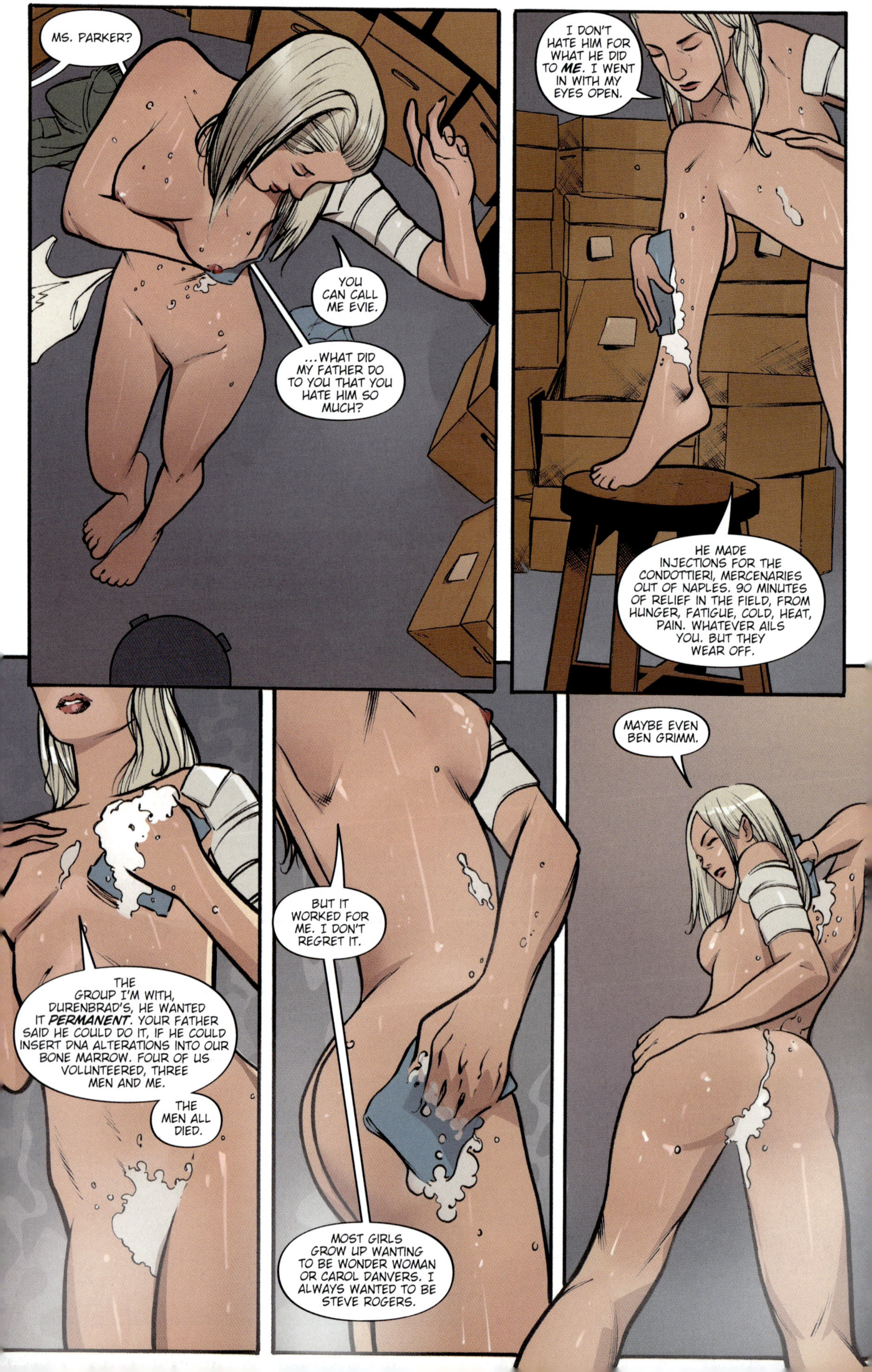
MS. PARKER?
YOU CAN CALL ME EVIE.
...WHAT DID MY FATHER DO TO YOU THAT YOU HATE HIM SO MUCH?
I DON'T HATE HIM FOR WHAT HE DID TO ME. I WENT IN WITH MY EYES OPEN.
HE MADE INJECTIONS FOR THE CONDOTTIERI, MERCENARIES OUT OF NAPLES. 90 MINUTES OF RELIEF IN THE FIELD, FROM HUNGER, FATIGUE, COLD, HEAT, PAIN. WHATEVER AILS YOU. BUT THEY WEAR OFF.
THE GROUP I'M WITH, DURENBRAD'S, HE WANTED IT PERMANENT. YOUR FATHER SAID HE COULD DO IT, IF HE COULD INSERT DNA ALTERATIONS INTO OUR BONE MARROW. FOUR OF US VOLUNTEERED, THREE MEN AND ME.
THE MEN ALL DIED.
BUT IT WORKED FOR ME. I DON'T REGRET IT.
MOST GIRLS GROW UP WANTING TO BE WONDER WOMAN OR CAROL DANVERS. I ALWAYS WANTED TO BE STEVE ROGERS.
MAYBE EVEN BEN GRIMM.

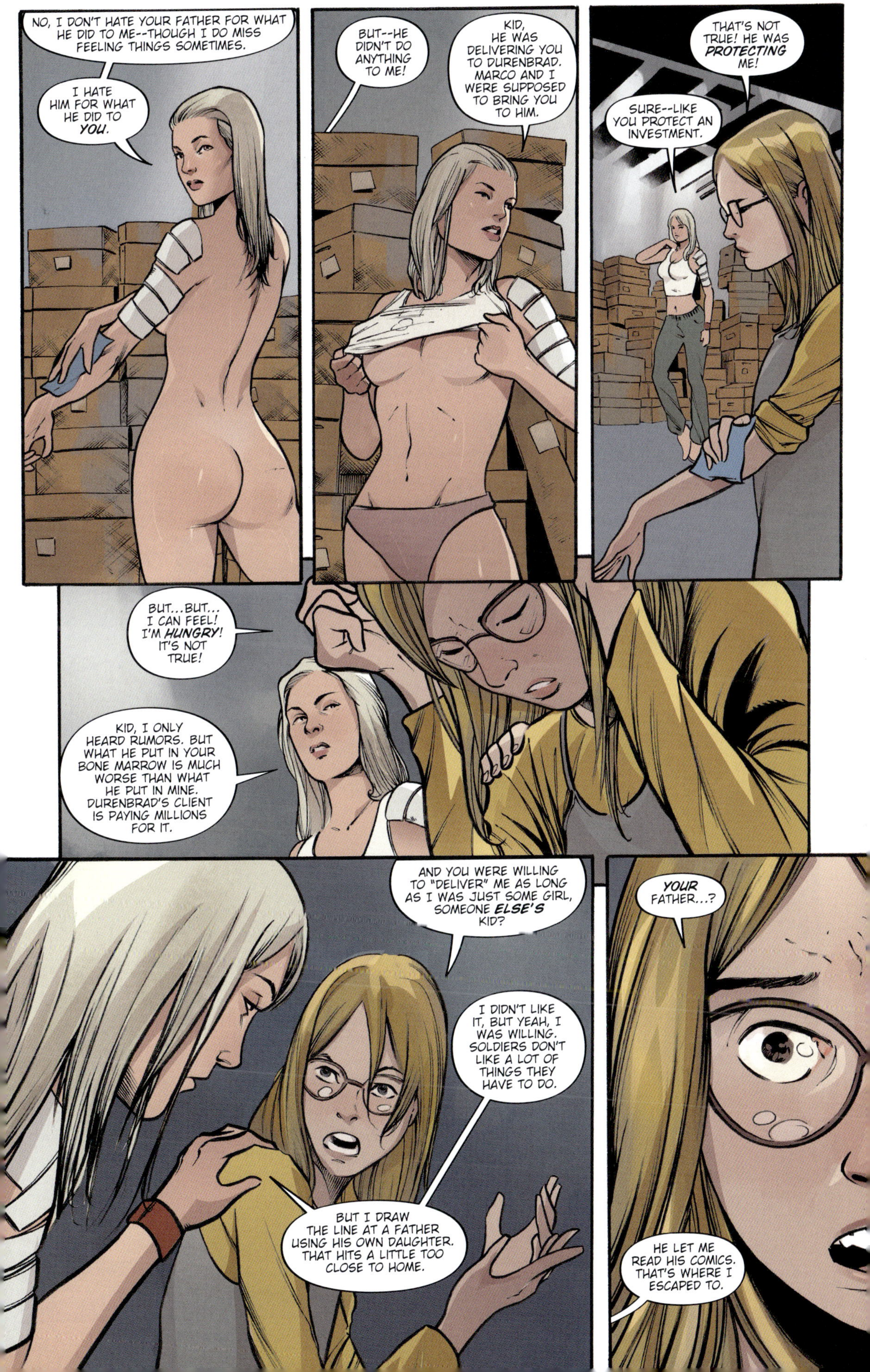
NO, I DON'T HATE YOUR FATHER FOR WHAT HE DID TO ME--THOUGH I DO MISS FEELING THINGS SOMETIMES.
I HATE HIM FOR WHAT HE DID TO *YOU*.
BUT--HE DIDN'T DO ANYTHING TO ME!
KID, HE WAS DELIVERING YOU TO DURENBRAD. MARCO AND I WERE SUPPOSED TO BRING YOU TO HIM.
THAT'S NOT TRUE! HE WAS *PROTECTING* ME!
SURE--LIKE YOU PROTECT AN INVESTMENT.
BUT...BUT... I CAN FEEL! I'M *HUNGRY*! IT'S NOT TRUE!
KID, I ONLY HEARD RUMORS. BUT WHAT HE PUT IN YOUR BONE MARROW IS MUCH WORSE THAN WHAT HE PUT IN MINE. DURENBRAD'S CLIENT IS PAYING MILLIONS FOR IT.
AND YOU WERE WILLING TO "DELIVER" ME AS LONG AS I WAS JUST SOME GIRL, SOMEONE *ELSE'S* KID?
I DIDN'T LIKE IT, BUT YEAH, I WAS WILLING. SOLDIERS DON'T LIKE A LOT OF THINGS THEY HAVE TO DO.
BUT I DRAW THE LINE AT A FATHER USING HIS OWN DAUGHTER. THAT HITS A LITTLE TOO CLOSE TO HOME.
YOUR FATHER...?
HE LET ME READ HIS COMICS. THAT'S WHERE I ESCAPED TO.

"ENOUGH QUESTIONS, KID. WE'RE GOING."

PROFESSOR. WORKING SATURDAYS, I SEE.

MM-HM.

VENICE, ITALY

APOP... APOPTOSIS. INDUCED APOPTOSIS. JESUS.

YOU *HAD* TO BE A THEATER MAJOR.

Phenotypic Conseq...
Apoptotic Proliferation...
By
Bessemer Preiss
& Livonia Cutler

PROFESSOR? WEREN'T YOU JUST...?

JUST WHAT, MATTEO?

JUST *HERE*...?

CLAK CLAK CLAK

GUARDS! THERE'S AN IMPOSTOR!

WHERE'S MY DAUGHTER? DO THE CONDOTTIERI HAVE HER?

THEY CAN'T DEPLOY WHAT I PUT IN HER WITHOUT KNOWING THE SCIENCE. IT'S USELESS TO THEM!

HE'S THE IMPOSTOR! HE TRIED TO KILL ME! I NEED AIR...

NOT ME-- IT'S HIM!

WHAT THE HELL...?

ARE YOU MAD? HE'S ESCAPING!

"YOU'VE GOT TO GO BACK TO VENICE, CESAR. WE NEED TO KNOW WHAT'S *REALLY* GOING ON."

"YOU'RE THINKING IF THE *NUNS* DIDN'T GIVE US UP, THE ONLY WAY THE KIDNAPPERS COULD GET TO THE CONVENT BEFORE US IS IF *PREISS* TOLD THEM WE WERE COMING?"

"EXACTLY. AND I DON'T ENJOY BEING LIED TO. ESPECIALLY BY THE PERSON I'M WORKING FOR."

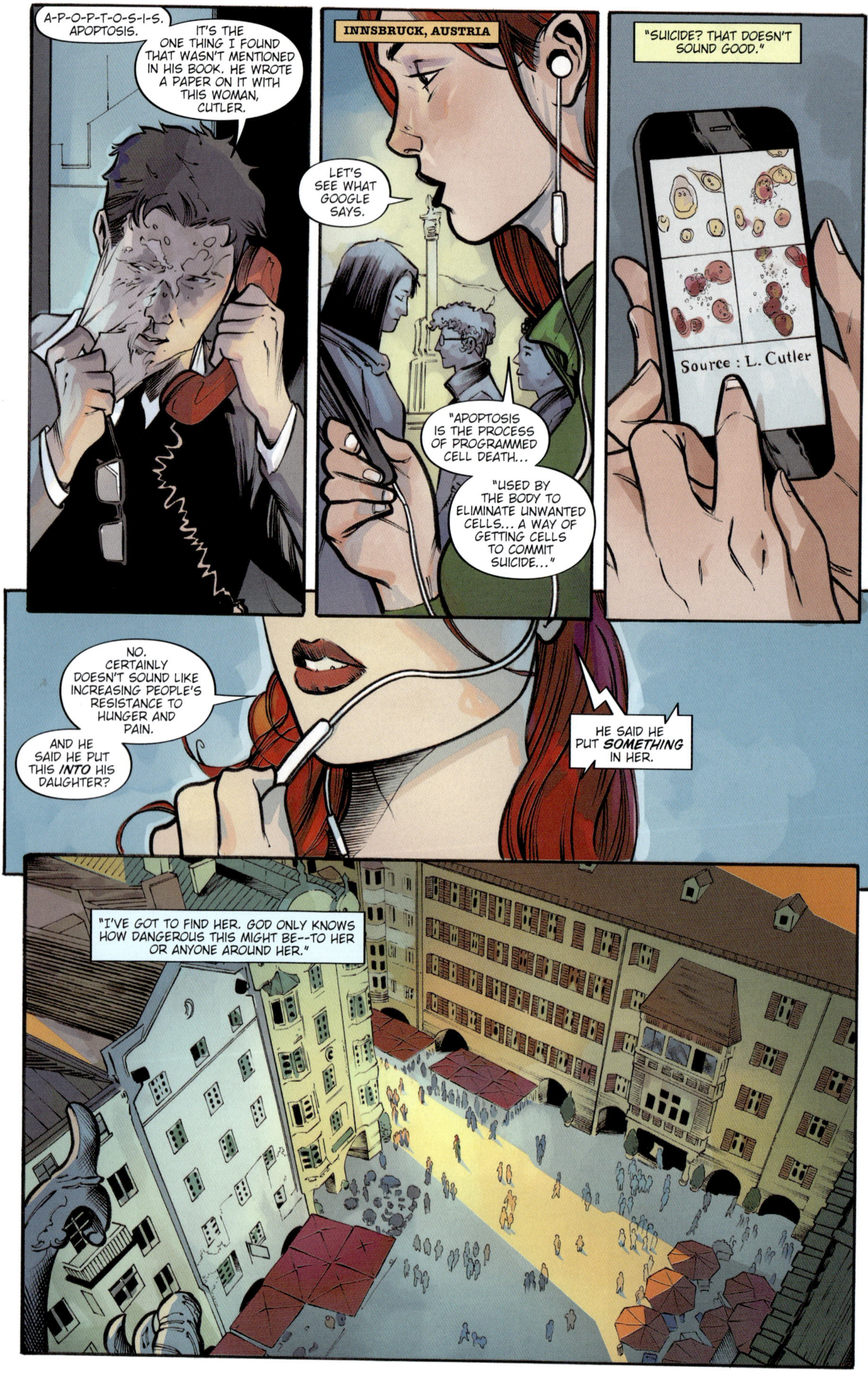
A-P-O-P-T-O-S-I-S. APOPTOSIS.
IT'S THE ONE THING I FOUND THAT WASN'T MENTIONED IN HIS BOOK. HE WROTE A PAPER ON IT WITH THIS WOMAN, CUTLER.
INNSBRUCK, AUSTRIA
LET'S SEE WHAT GOOGLE SAYS.
"APOPTOSIS IS THE PROCESS OF PROGRAMMED CELL DEATH...
"USED BY THE BODY TO ELIMINATE UNWANTED CELLS... A WAY OF GETTING CELLS TO COMMIT SUICIDE..."
"SUICIDE? THAT DOESN'T SOUND GOOD."
Source : L. Cutler
NO. CERTAINLY DOESN'T SOUND LIKE INCREASING PEOPLE'S RESISTANCE TO HUNGER AND PAIN.
AND HE SAID HE PUT THIS *INTO* HIS DAUGHTER?
HE SAID HE PUT *SOMETHING* IN HER.
"I'VE GOT TO FIND HER. GOD ONLY KNOWS HOW DANGEROUS THIS MIGHT BE--TO HER OR ANYONE AROUND HER."

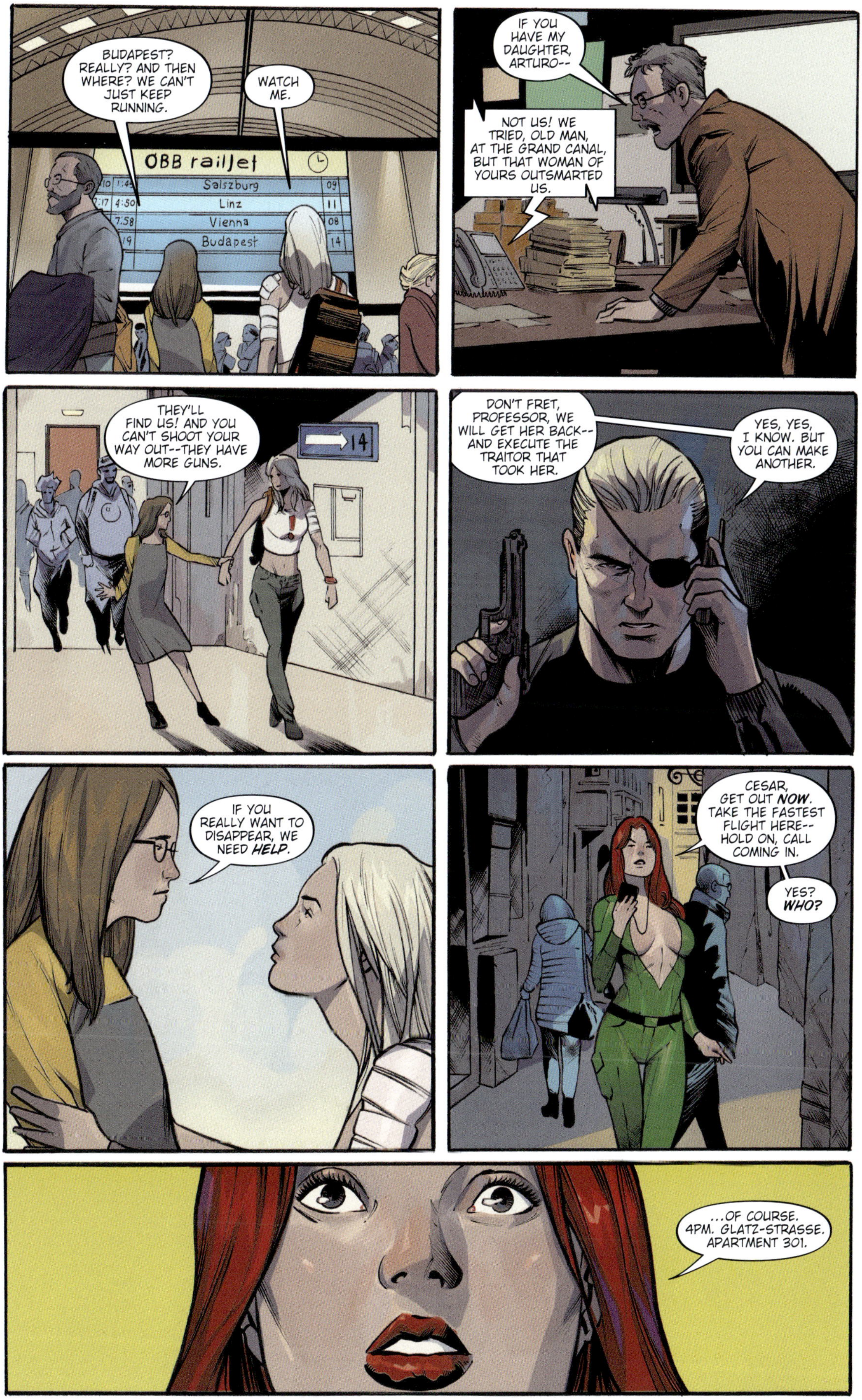
BUDAPEST? REALLY? AND THEN WHERE? WE CAN'T JUST KEEP RUNNING.
WATCH ME.
ÖBB railjet
Salszburg
Linz
Vienna
Budapest
IF YOU HAVE MY DAUGHTER, ARTURO--
NOT US! WE TRIED, OLD MAN, AT THE GRAND CANAL, BUT THAT WOMAN OF YOURS OUTSMARTED US.
THEY'LL FIND US! AND YOU CAN'T SHOOT YOUR WAY OUT--THEY HAVE MORE GUNS.
14
DON'T FRET, PROFESSOR, WE WILL GET HER BACK--AND EXECUTE THE TRAITOR THAT TOOK HER.
YES, YES, I KNOW. BUT YOU CAN MAKE ANOTHER.
IF YOU REALLY WANT TO DISAPPEAR, WE NEED *HELP*.
CESAR, GET OUT *NOW*. TAKE THE FASTEST FLIGHT HERE--HOLD ON, CALL COMING IN.
YES? *WHO?*
...OF COURSE. 4PM. GLATZ-STRASSE. APARTMENT 301.

MS. RACERS, THIS IS EVIE.

SHE'S A FRIEND.

WE WANT TO HIRE YOU TO HELP US DISAPPEAR.

Model: Grace McClung

CHAPTER THREE

Illustrated by:
Kendrick Lim

GENTLEMEN, WE HAVE AN UNEXPLODED BOMB ON THE STREETS OF INNSBRUCK, AUSTRIA.
THIS 12-YEAR-OLD GIRL, ROSALINE PREISS.
SHE HAS NO IDEA WHAT SHE'S CARRYING AROUND IN HER BONE MARROW. ONCE ACTIVATED, IT COULD KILL ANY LIVING ORGANISM ON THE PLANET.
WE NEED HER *ALIVE*. YOUR FORMER COLLEAGUE WHO IS HELPING HER, NOT SO MUCH.
RECALL THAT PARKER FEELS NO PAIN, NO HUNGER, NO FATIGUE. DON'T TAKE ANY CHANCES. IF YOU ENCOUNTER HER...

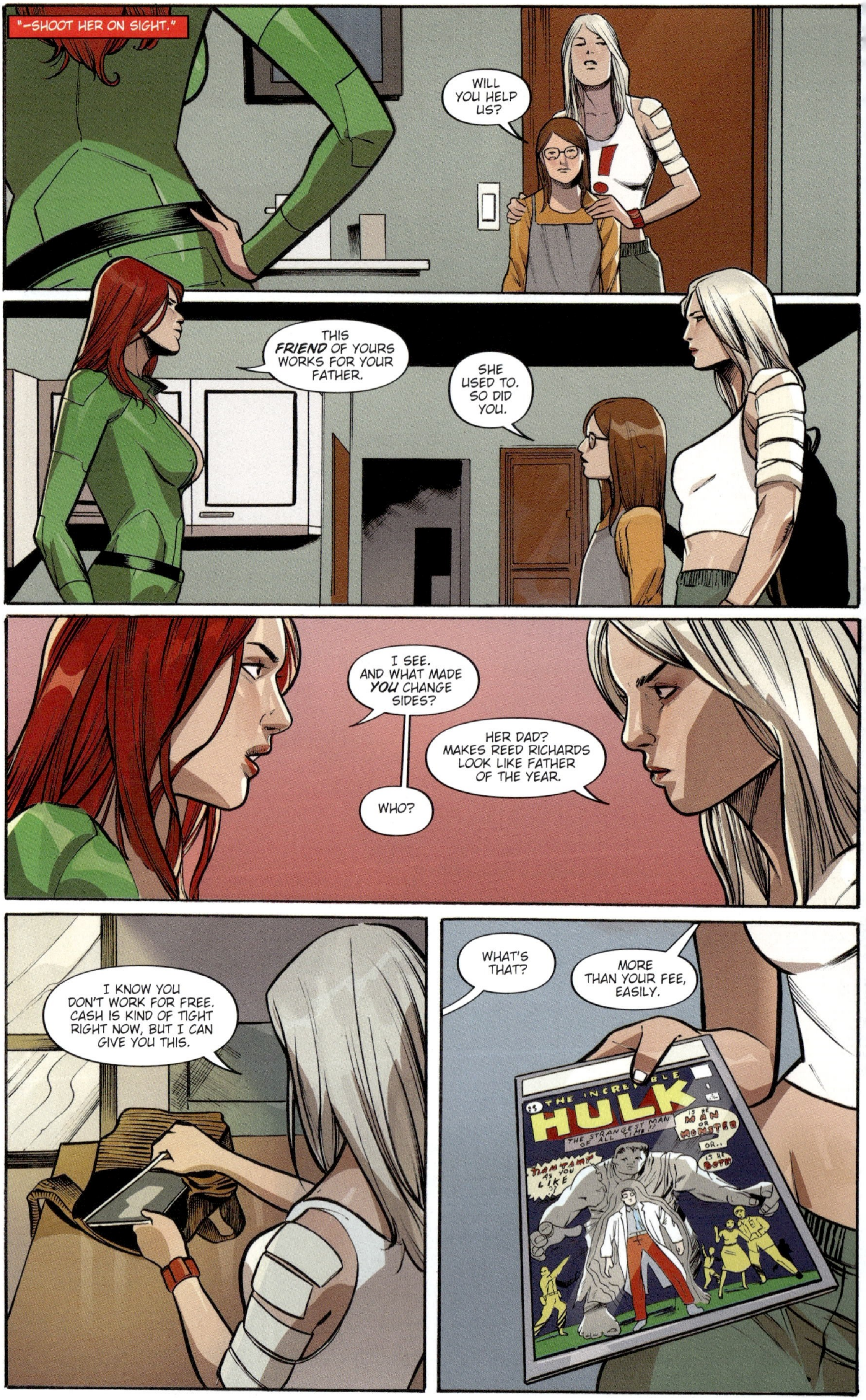
"–SHOOT HER ON SIGHT."
WILL YOU HELP US?
THIS *FRIEND* OF YOURS WORKS FOR YOUR FATHER.
SHE USED TO. SO DID YOU.
I SEE. AND WHAT MADE *YOU* CHANGE SIDES?
HER DAD? MAKES REED RICHARDS LOOK LIKE FATHER OF THE YEAR.
WHO?
I KNOW YOU DON'T WORK FOR FREE. CASH IS KIND OF TIGHT RIGHT NOW, BUT I CAN GIVE YOU THIS.
WHAT'S THAT?
MORE THAN YOUR FEE, EASILY.
HULK

LET'S SAY I AGREE TO HELP--NOT FOR YOUR SAKE, FOR HERS.
YOU'LL BOTH HAVE TO DO **EXACTLY** AS I TELL YOU, EVEN IF YOU DON'T UNDERSTAND WHY--EVEN IF YOU DON'T AGREE.
I'M A SOLDIER. I KNOW HOW TO FOLLOW ORDERS.
YOU USED TO.
TRY THIS ON.
YOU'VE GOT THE TOUGHER JOB. REMEMBER CESAR, FROM VENICE? WELL, THIS TIME YOU'RE GOING TO NEED TO LOOK LIKE **HIM**. AND THAT MEANS--SHORT HAIR.
DO I **HAVE** TO?
I'M SORRY, KID. THESE PEOPLE AREN'T PLAYING AROUND. YOU CAN BE A LIVE BOY OR A DEAD GIRL.
DO IT.
JUST SEND IT TO LOCKS OF LOVE, OK...?

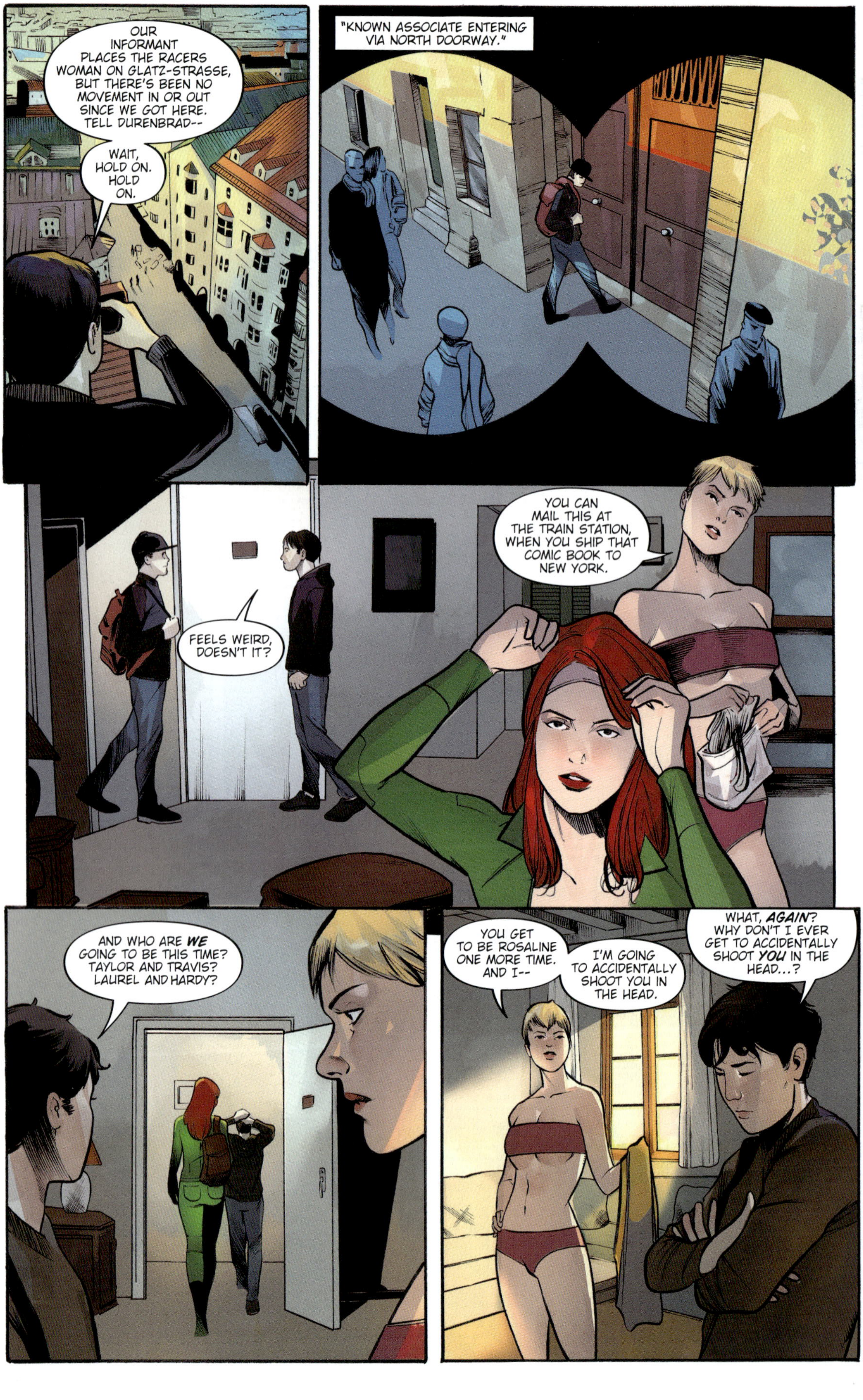
OUR INFORMANT PLACES THE RACERS WOMAN ON GLATZ-STRASSE, BUT THERE'S BEEN NO MOVEMENT IN OR OUT SINCE WE GOT HERE. TELL DURENBRAD--
WAIT, HOLD ON. HOLD ON.
"KNOWN ASSOCIATE ENTERING VIA NORTH DOORWAY."
FEELS WEIRD, DOESN'T IT?
YOU CAN MAIL THIS AT THE TRAIN STATION, WHEN YOU SHIP THAT COMIC BOOK TO NEW YORK.
AND WHO ARE WE GOING TO BE THIS TIME? TAYLOR AND TRAVIS? LAUREL AND HARDY?
YOU GET TO BE ROSALINE ONE MORE TIME. AND I--
I'M GOING TO ACCIDENTALLY SHOOT YOU IN THE HEAD.
WHAT, AGAIN? WHY DON'T I EVER GET TO ACCIDENTALLY SHOOT YOU IN THE HEAD...?

RACERS IS ON THE MOVE.
"USE THE TICKETS YOU'VE ALREADY GOT. WE'LL BRING THE DOCTOR TO YOU--WILLINGLY, HOPEFULLY; AT GUNPOINT IF NECESSARY."
ÖBB
P
WE CAN'T MAKE IT TO THE GATE. CAN'T RISK THEM QUESTIONING US.
AUSGANG
EXIT
SORTIE
BUT THEY WON'T RECOGNIZE US NOW!
THEY KNOW MY VOICE
THEN WHAT DO WE DO? MS. RACERS SAID--
WE'LL DO WHAT SHE SAID--ONCE SHE'S DRAWN SOME OF THE HEAT AWAY.

DURENBRAD.
I HAVE MORE THAN JUST YOUR NUMBER. I HAVE YOUR GIRL.
HOW DID YOU GET THIS NUMBER?
YOU'RE FULL OF SHIT. MY MEN HAVE EYES ON YOU. YOU'RE AT THE--
--LAUFHAUS BY THE TRAIN STATION. REPEAT: RACERS AND HER MAN HAVE GONE INSIDE. NO SIGN OF THE GIRL OR PARKER.
YOU WANT TWO GIRLS OR JUST ONE?
ONE. AND IF ANYONE ELSE COMES IN, TELL THEM THE STEAM ROOM IS IN USE. OFF-LIMITS, UNDERSTAND?
IF YOU STILL HAVE A MAN WATCHING AT GLATZ-STRASSE, ASK HIM WHAT HE SEES AT THE WINDOW.
NOW, THAT'S GOING TO COST YOU EXTRA.
IT'S NOT FOR YOU. JUST HANG OUT WITH MY FRIEND, AND DON'T TALK TO HIM--HE DOESN'T SPEAK ANY GERMAN.
WARP FACTOR 9, CAPTAIN.
TELL THE MEN TO GO IN AND GET RACERS NOW. I'LL TAKE GLATZ-STRASSE MYSELF.
IT COULD BE A TRAP, SIR.
OF COURSE IT'S A TRAP.

ENGLISCH? FRANÇAIS...?
YOU ARE SURE YOU DO NOT WANT I SHOULD DO ANYTHING?
UM, NO. THANKS.
BLAM!
STEAM ROOM IT IS.
JESUS--IT'S AN OVEN!
GET OUT OF THERE! YOU TRYING TO KILL YOURSELVES?
OH, BECKER, YOU ASSHOLE. COULD'VE GUESSED HE'D SEND YOU.

WELL, BOYS, IT SEEMS TO BE CLOBBERIN' TIME.

WHAAAP!

WHAM
WHOOF
KRAK
GET OUR STUFF, KID. WE'RE LEAVING.
NOT SO FAST.
NEITHER OF YOU IS GOING ANYWHERE.
I'LL KILL YOU IF YOU HURT HER.
"HER"?

THAT'S NOT HER.
IT'S A PROJECTION, IT'S A DUMMY, A CARDBOARD CUTOUT--IT'S SOMETHING, BUT IT'S NOT THE GIRL. THEY WOULDN'T JUST LEAVE HER THERE, STANDING AT A WINDOW.
WANT BACKUP?
NO. THIS IS A ONE-MAN OPERATION. ONE MAN READY TO SHOOT ANYTHING THAT MOVES.
THEY COULD HAVE THE PLACE BOOBY-TRAPPED, WIRED TO BLOW.
WE'LL FIND OUT.

BLAM!

CLEAR!

GET PLENTY OF BLOOD ON THAT THING AND WE'LL WRAP YOU UP.

DON'T DO IT, GEORG.
PARKER...?
OUR ORDERS ARE TO SHOOT YOU ON SIGHT.
MY ORDERS IN RAQQA WERE TO LEAVE YOU BEHIND.
AND WHOSE BLOOD IS THAT? BECKER? HIRSCH?
I'M SORRY, PARKER. I ALWAYS LIKED YOU.
DA BLAMM!
NO!

BOOOOOM!
GET THE CAR, QUICK!
THE GIRL'S BEEN HIT.
SO IT WAS HER?
SHE HASN'T GOT LONG. GET HER TO DR. CUTLER IMMEDIATELY.
NO COMMUNICATION WITH ANYONE BUT ME. DON'T STOP FOR ANYTHING. IF SHE DIES BEFORE WE CAN GET THE STUFF OUT OF HER, I'LL SHOOT YOU MYSELF.
YES, SIR!

EITHER YOU'RE DAHLIA AND YOU SLIPPED A TRACKER IN MY BAG OR I'M FUCKED.

WHAT? DON'T LIKE SEEING YOURSELF SHOT...?
WHERE'S ROSALINE?
I'LL GET HER BACK.
I'LL GET HER. YOU'VE GOT A BULLET INSIDE YOU. I DON'T EVEN KNOW WHY YOU'RE STILL ALIVE.
JUST GOT LUCKY. IT'S NOT A WOLVERINE THING, I DON'T HEAL QUICK.
HELPS THAT I CAN'T FEEL IT, THOUGH.

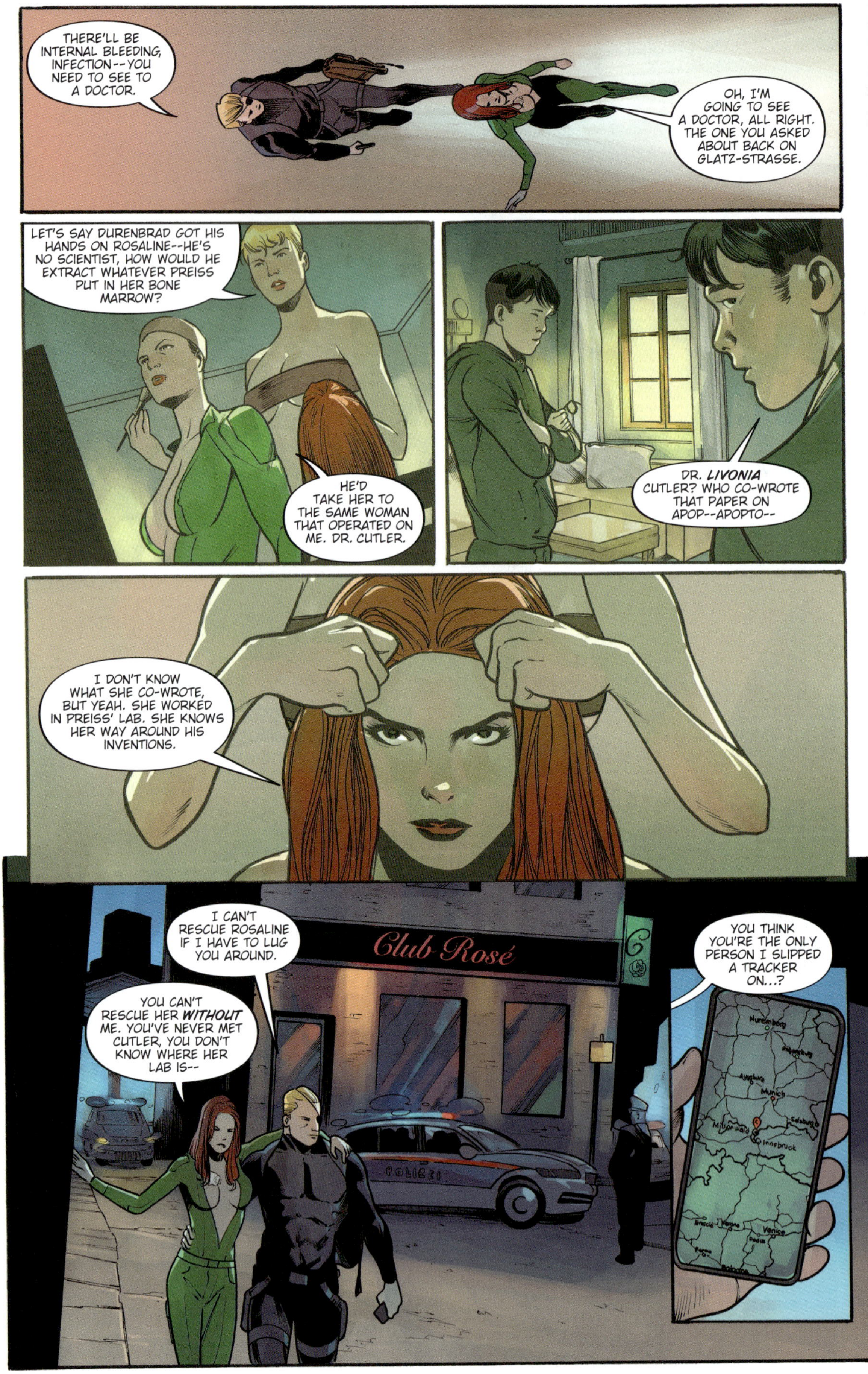
THERE'LL BE INTERNAL BLEEDING, INFECTION--YOU NEED TO SEE TO A DOCTOR.
OH, I'M GOING TO SEE A DOCTOR, ALL RIGHT. THE ONE YOU ASKED ABOUT BACK ON GLATZ-STRASSE.
LET'S SAY DURENBRAD GOT HIS HANDS ON ROSALINE--HE'S NO SCIENTIST, HOW WOULD HE EXTRACT WHATEVER PREISS PUT IN HER BONE MARROW?
HE'D TAKE HER TO THE SAME WOMAN THAT OPERATED ON ME. DR. CUTLER.
DR. LIVONIA CUTLER? WHO CO-WROTE THAT PAPER ON APOP--APOPTO--
I DON'T KNOW WHAT SHE CO-WROTE, BUT YEAH. SHE WORKED IN PREISS' LAB. SHE KNOWS HER WAY AROUND HIS INVENTIONS.
Club Rosé
I CAN'T RESCUE ROSALINE IF I HAVE TO LUG YOU AROUND.
YOU CAN'T RESCUE HER WITHOUT ME. YOU'VE NEVER MET CUTLER, YOU DON'T KNOW WHERE HER LAB IS--
POLIZEI
YOU THINK YOU'RE THE ONLY PERSON I SLIPPED A TRACKER ON...?
Nuremberg
Augsburg
Munich
Salzburg
Innsbruck
Venice

4.6 KM SOUTH OF MITTENWALD, GERMANY.
DR. CUTLER!
YOU'LL NEED HELP WHEN YOU GET THERE.
I'VE GOT HELP WHEN I GET THERE.
YOU'LL NEED MORE.
A SECOND ONE. FASCINATING.
PLEASE. LET ME COME.
YOU REALLY CARE ABOUT HER, DON'T YOU?
YOU MEET A NEWT, IT BRINGS OUT THE RIPLEY IN YOU.
DURENBRAD'S ORDERS--
I KNOW HIS ORDERS. YOU CAN GO NOW.
YES, MA'AM.
I SAID, YOU'RE DISMISSED.

IF YOU HAVE A GUN UNDER THOSE BANDAGES, YOU CAN USE IT ON ME IF YOU LIKE--BUT THE GIRL WILL DIE IF YOU DO.
I CAME HERE TO GET YOUR HELP--BUT I THINK IT'S WHAT YOU'RE ALREADY DOING, TAKING THAT STUFF OUT OF HER.
YOU HAVE NO IDEA WHAT I'M DOING. NO IDEA WHAT'S AT STAKE.
'INDUCED APOPTOSIS'?
YOU DON'T EVEN KNOW HOW TO SAY THE WORD. THE SECOND 'P' IS SILENT.
NO OFFENSE, BUT CAN WE SKIP THE SCRABBLE DICTIONARY? THERE'S A MAN OUTSIDE WITH A BIGGER GUN THAN MINE, AND I STILL DON'T KNOW WHOSE SIDE YOU'RE ON.

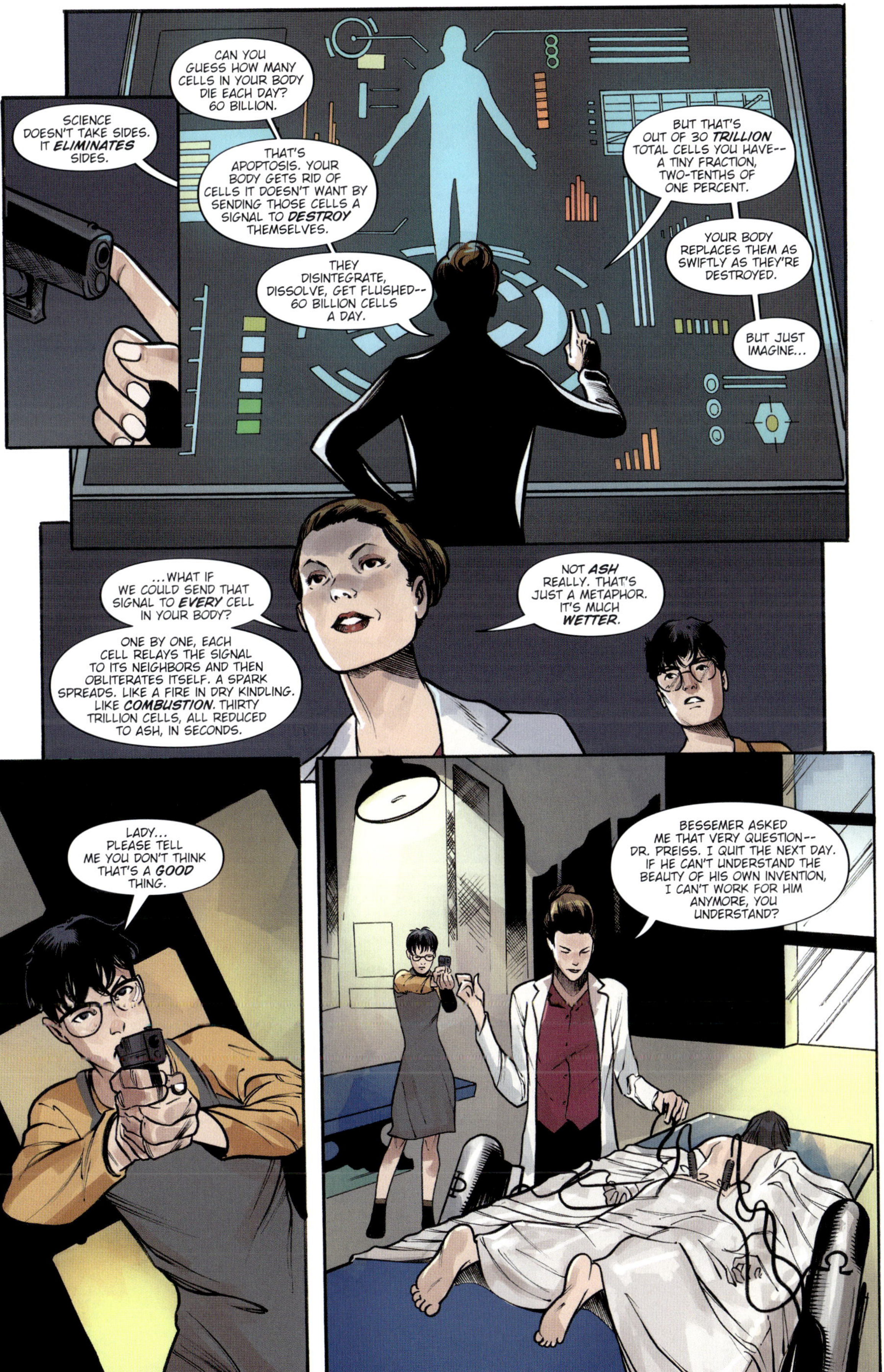
SCIENCE DOESN'T TAKE SIDES. IT ELIMINATES SIDES.
CAN YOU GUESS HOW MANY CELLS IN YOUR BODY DIE EACH DAY? 60 BILLION.
THAT'S APOPTOSIS. YOUR BODY GETS RID OF CELLS IT DOESN'T WANT BY SENDING THOSE CELLS A SIGNAL TO DESTROY THEMSELVES.
THEY DISINTEGRATE, DISSOLVE, GET FLUSHED-- 60 BILLION CELLS A DAY.
BUT THAT'S OUT OF 30 TRILLION TOTAL CELLS YOU HAVE-- A TINY FRACTION, TWO-TENTHS OF ONE PERCENT.
YOUR BODY REPLACES THEM AS SWIFTLY AS THEY'RE DESTROYED.
BUT JUST IMAGINE...
...WHAT IF WE COULD SEND THAT SIGNAL TO EVERY CELL IN YOUR BODY?
ONE BY ONE, EACH CELL RELAYS THE SIGNAL TO ITS NEIGHBORS AND THEN OBLITERATES ITSELF. A SPARK SPREADS. LIKE A FIRE IN DRY KINDLING. LIKE COMBUSTION. THIRTY TRILLION CELLS, ALL REDUCED TO ASH, IN SECONDS.
NOT ASH REALLY. THAT'S JUST A METAPHOR. IT'S MUCH WETTER.
LADY... PLEASE TELL ME YOU DON'T THINK THAT'S A GOOD THING.
BESSEMER ASKED ME THAT VERY QUESTION-- DR. PREISS. I QUIT THE NEXT DAY. IF HE CAN'T UNDERSTAND THE BEAUTY OF HIS OWN INVENTION, I CAN'T WORK FOR HIM ANYMORE, YOU UNDERSTAND?

YES, SIR... SHE ORDERED ME OUT OF THE ROOM... YES, THE GIRL'S ALIVE...
HOLD YOUR POSITION, WE'RE ALMOST THERE.
GOT ANY HANDCUFFS IN THAT BAG OF YOURS?
...DON'T WORRY, CHEWIE, I THINK I KNOW WHAT HE HAS IN MIND.
YOU'RE SAYING YOU CAN'T TAKE THOSE TUBES OUT OF HER WITHOUT TURNING HER TO ASH?
NOT WHILE THIS PROCESS IS GOING ON.
PARKER'S DEAD. I GOT THIS ONE. SHE MAY HAVE INFORMATION THE DOCTOR NEEDS.
YOU STAY HERE AND WATCH FOR TROUBLE. NO TELLING WHO MIGHT SHOW UP.
BESSEMER WRAPPED THE APOPTOTIC AGENT IN AN ANTIBODY JACKET--THAT'S WHY IT HASN'T HARMED HER. IT'S ONLY ACTIVATED WHEN THE JACKET IS SEPARATED FROM THE AGENT, A VERY DELICATE OPERATION.
IF WE INTERRUPT IT, THERE WON'T BE ENOUGH LEFT OF HER TO FILL A BUCKET.
AND ONCE IT'S DONE, WHAT LUCKY CLIENT OF DURENBRAD'S GETS TO BUY THIS LETHAL NEW CHEMICAL AGENT?
THERE'S NO CLIENT. DURENBRAD'S A FOOL. I'M GOING TO USE IT--THE ANTIBODY TO GIVE OUR OWN MEN IMMUNITY, SO THEY CAN DO THEIR WORK, AND THE AGENT...
THE AGENT WILL BE FIELD-TESTED IN A DENSE POPULATION CENTER SO I CAN STUDY THE SPREAD AND CONTAINMENT.

WHAT POPULATION CENTER?
THERE WERE SEVERAL GOOD CANDIDATES. BAGHDAD, HONG KONG. WUHAN. IN THE END I SETTLED ON LONDON.
RIGHT SIZE, GOOD GEOGRAPHY--AND DOING IT THERE WILL GET ATTENTION. IN ALL, APPROXIMATELY EIGHT MILLION PEOPLE WILL BE AFFECTED.
"AFFECTED"? YOU MEAN *KILLED*. YOU'D SLAUGHTER EIGHT MILLION PEOPLE?
OUT OF A WORLD POPULATION OF EIGHT *BILLION*? THAT'S *ONE* TENTH OF ONE PERCENT--HALF AS MUCH AS YOUR BODY ELIMINATES EVERY DAY IN UNWANTED CELLS.
OUR PLANET IS *DYING*. WHEN I WAS BORN, IT HELD ONLY FOUR BILLION PEOPLE. IN MY LIFETIME ALONE IT HAS DOUBLED.
EIGHT MILLION IS NOTHING. *EIGHT HUNDRED MILLION* WOULD BARELY BE A START.
WHY ARE YOU TELLING ME ALL THIS?
YOU'RE GOING TO BE MY MESSENGER. ONCE YOU LEARN TO PRONOUNCE THE FUCKING WORD RIGHT.
PSSHH
GET AWAY FROM HER, YOU *BITCH*.
IT'S OVER. LET HER GO.

BLAM!
OVER? IT'S JUST BEGUN.
HEY! WHO THE HELL ARE YOU? THEY JUST FOUND A BURNED BODY ON GLATZ-STRASSE--
BLAM!
DRAVES! DRAVES...! REINFORCEMENTS HEADED YOUR WAY, DO YOU COPY?
SHIT.

Model: Grace McClung

CHAPTER FOUR

Illustrated by:
Ivan Tao

"CUTLER'S ON THAT PLANE. SHE'S GOT TO BE."

THE QUESTION IS, DID SHE TAKE ROSALINE AND CESAR WITH HER?

THE *QUESTION* IS HOW DO WE *FOLLOW* THEM NOW-- UNLESS THAT CAR OF YOURS IS SECRETLY A DELOREAN.

NO. BUT I'M BETTING NO ONE WOULD BUILD A RUNWAY LIKE THAT FOR JUST ONE PLANE.

CESAR! HOW MANY ON THE PLANE?
THE PROFESSOR'S WEAPON--?
CUTLER VACUUMED IT OUT OF HER. SHE'S ***UNHINGED.*** WANTS TO KILL HALF THE PEOPLE ON THE PLANET, STARTING WITH EVERYONE IN LONDON.
HELLO, THANOS.
AND SCORSESE SAYS THE MCU ISN'T REALISTIC.
WHAT'S WITH ***HER***?
GOT SHOT IN THE CHEST. BULLET'S STILL IN THERE.
HEY, PARKER--IF YOU NEED TO BOW OUT, NOW'S THE TIME. CESAR CAN DRIVE YOU TO A HOSPITAL, I'LL FIGURE OUT HOW TO FLY THIS THING.

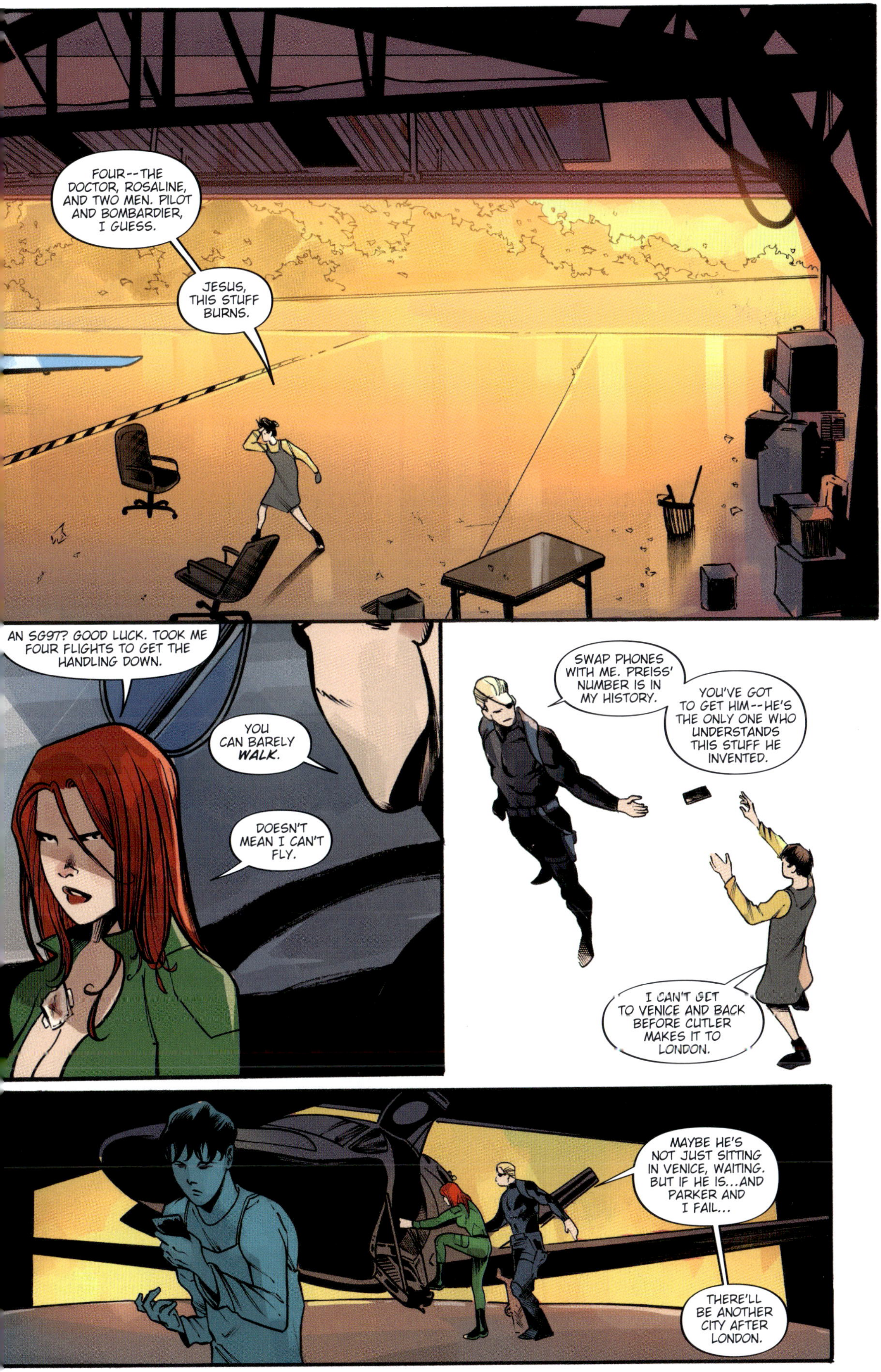
FOUR--THE DOCTOR, ROSALINE, AND TWO MEN. PILOT AND BOMBARDIER, I GUESS.
JESUS, THIS STUFF BURNS.
AN SG97? GOOD LUCK. TOOK ME FOUR FLIGHTS TO GET THE HANDLING DOWN.
YOU CAN BARELY *WALK*.
DOESN'T MEAN I CAN'T FLY.
SWAP PHONES WITH ME. PREISS' NUMBER IS IN MY HISTORY.
YOU'VE GOT TO GET HIM--HE'S THE ONLY ONE WHO UNDERSTANDS THIS STUFF HE INVENTED.
I CAN'T GET TO VENICE AND BACK BEFORE CUTLER MAKES IT TO LONDON.
MAYBE HE'S NOT JUST SITTING IN VENICE, WAITING. BUT IF HE IS...AND PARKER AND I FAIL...
THERE'LL BE ANOTHER CITY AFTER LONDON.

YOU'VE FILLED THE TANKS, LITTLE ONE. YOU CAN REST--AND START MAKING MORE.
BZZZ... BZZZ...
B. Preiss
NOW YOU WANT TO TALK. TOO LITTLE, TOO LATE, BESSEMER.
PREPARED FOR YOUR JUMP, MR. STECKLER?
ON IT.
WHEN DO WE GET OUR SHOTS, DOC?
NOT TILL THE LAST SECOND. THE PROTECTION ONLY LASTS ABOUT 90 MINUTES, AND WE WILL NEED EVERY ONE OF THEM.
NOTIFY ME WHEN WE'VE PASSED GRAVESEND, MR. BRAUN.

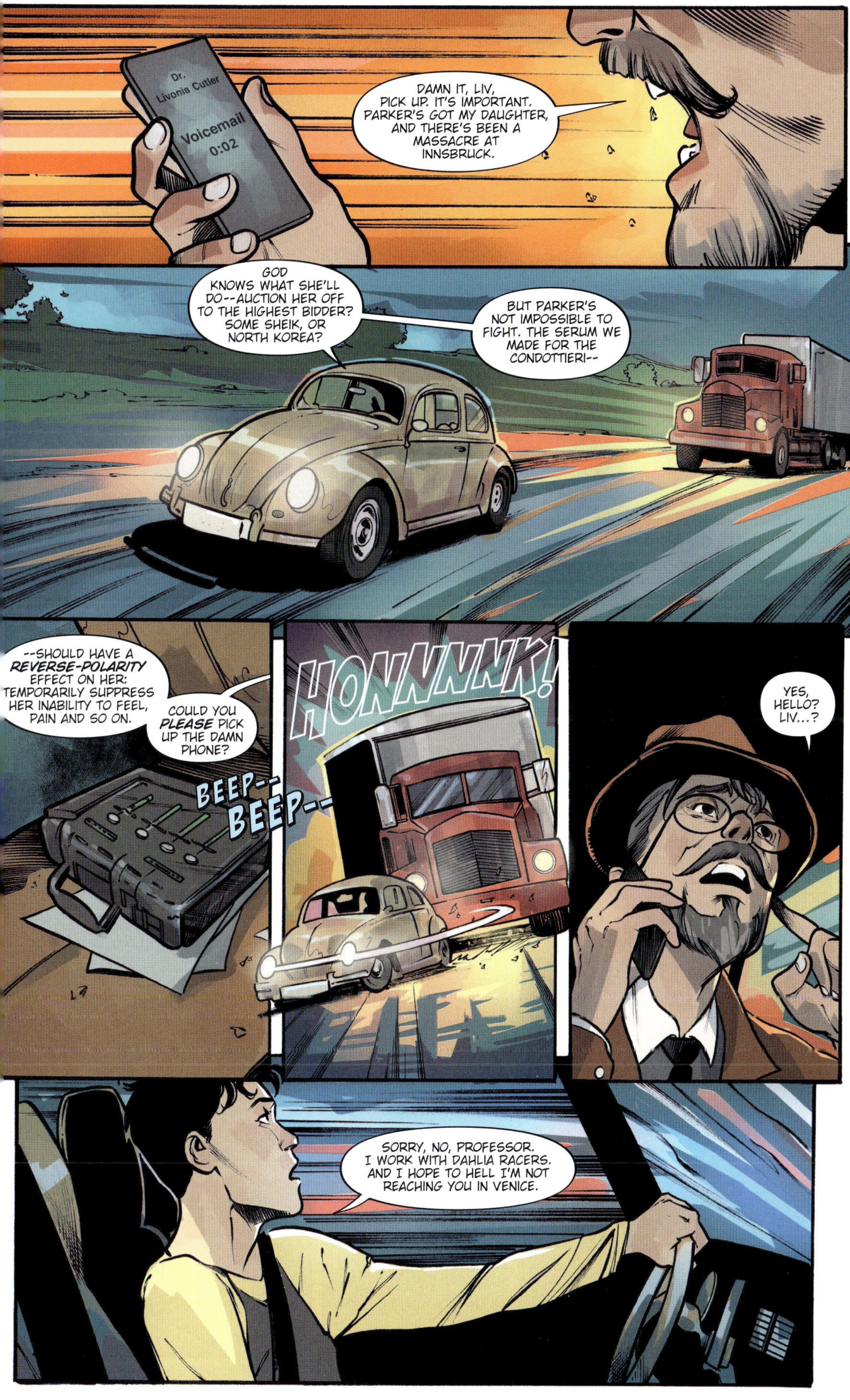
Dr.
Livonia Cutler
Voicemail
0:02
DAMN IT, LIV, PICK UP. IT'S IMPORTANT. PARKER'S GOT MY DAUGHTER, AND THERE'S BEEN A MASSACRE AT INNSBRUCK.
GOD KNOWS WHAT SHE'LL DO--AUCTION HER OFF TO THE HIGHEST BIDDER? SOME SHEIK, OR NORTH KOREA?
BUT PARKER'S NOT IMPOSSIBLE TO FIGHT. THE SERUM WE MADE FOR THE CONDOTTIERI--
--SHOULD HAVE A ***REVERSE-POLARITY*** EFFECT ON HER: TEMPORARILY SUPPRESS HER INABILITY TO FEEL, PAIN AND SO ON.
COULD YOU ***PLEASE*** PICK UP THE DAMN PHONE?
BEEP--
BEEP--
HONNNNK!
YES, HELLO? LIV...?
SORRY, NO, PROFESSOR. I WORK WITH DAHLIA RACERS. AND I HOPE TO HELL I'M NOT REACHING YOU IN VENICE.

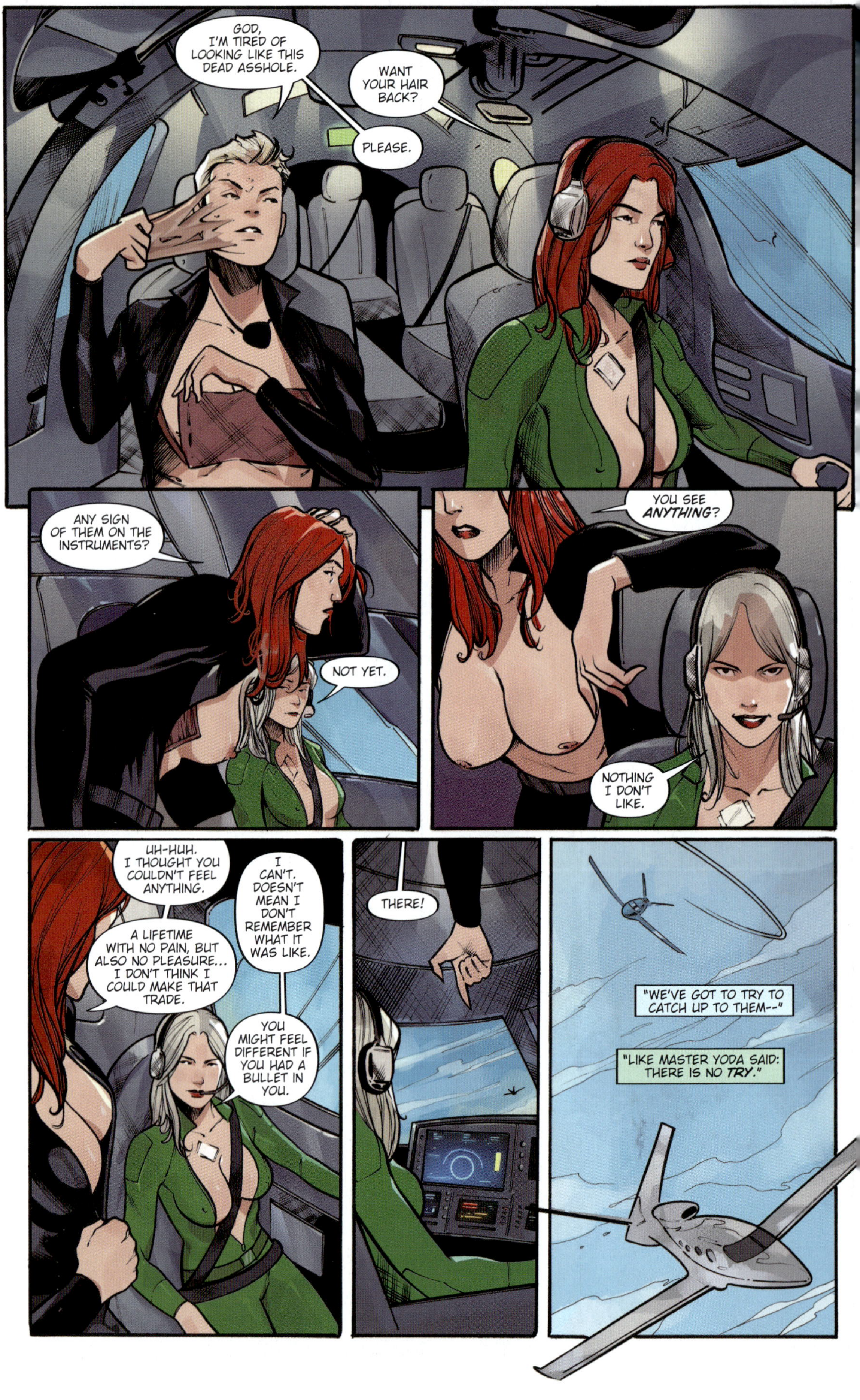
GOD, I'M TIRED OF LOOKING LIKE THIS DEAD ASSHOLE.
WANT YOUR HAIR BACK?
PLEASE.
ANY SIGN OF THEM ON THE INSTRUMENTS?
NOT YET.
YOU SEE *ANYTHING*?
NOTHING I DON'T LIKE.
UH-HUH. I THOUGHT YOU COULDN'T FEEL ANYTHING.
I CAN'T. DOESN'T MEAN I DON'T REMEMBER WHAT IT WAS LIKE.
A LIFETIME WITH NO PAIN, BUT ALSO NO PLEASURE... I DON'T THINK I COULD MAKE THAT TRADE.
YOU MIGHT FEEL DIFFERENT IF YOU HAD A BULLET IN YOU.
THERE!
"WE'VE GOT TO TRY TO CATCH UP TO THEM--"
"LIKE MASTER YODA SAID: THERE IS NO *TRY*."

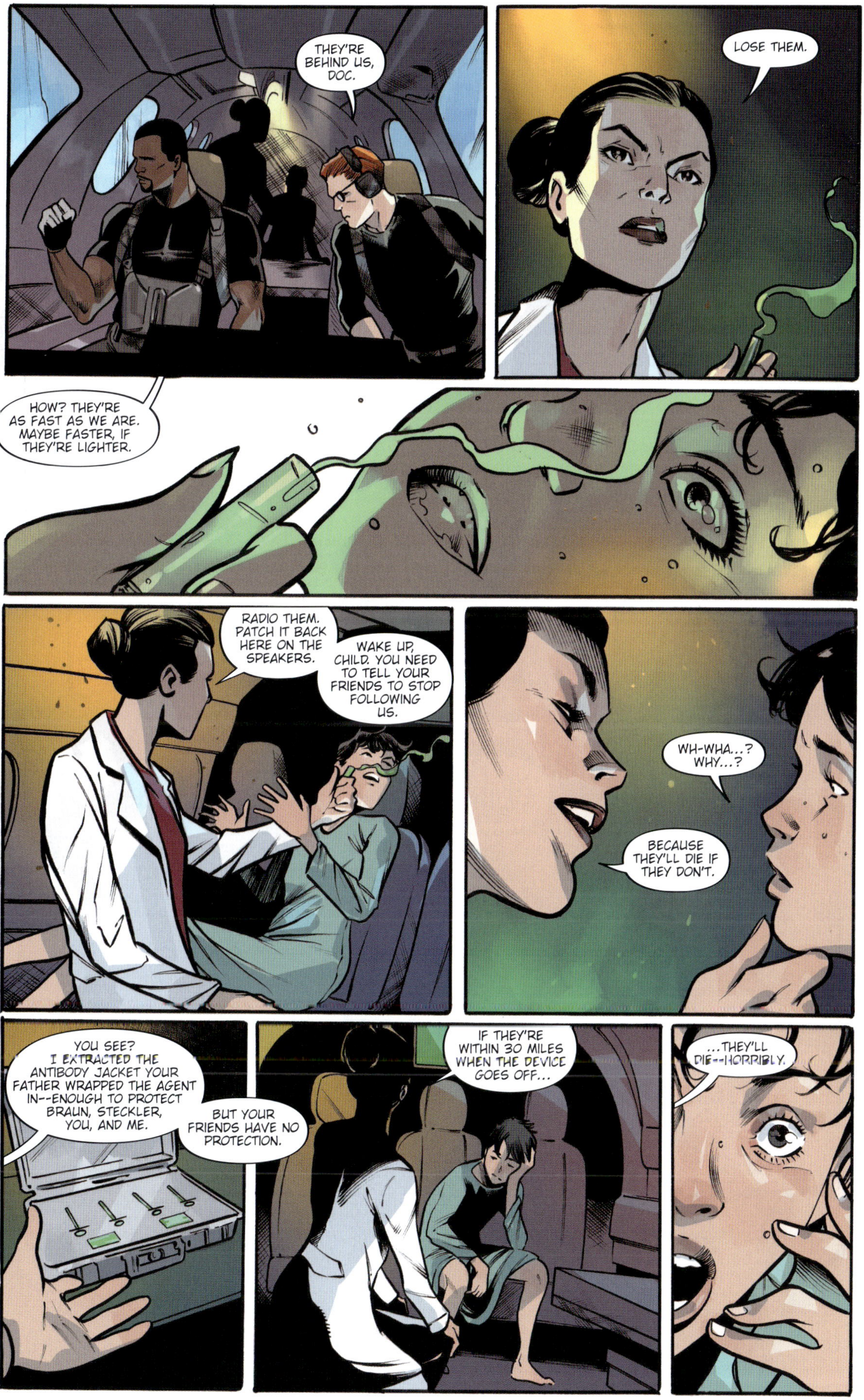
THEY'RE BEHIND US, DOC.
LOSE THEM.
HOW? THEY'RE AS FAST AS WE ARE. MAYBE FASTER, IF THEY'RE LIGHTER.
RADIO THEM. PATCH IT BACK HERE ON THE SPEAKERS.
WAKE UP, CHILD. YOU NEED TO TELL YOUR FRIENDS TO STOP FOLLOWING US.
WH-WHA...? WHY...?
BECAUSE THEY'LL DIE IF THEY DON'T.
YOU SEE? I EXTRACTED THE ANTIBODY JACKET YOUR FATHER WRAPPED THE AGENT IN--ENOUGH TO PROTECT BRAUN, STECKLER, YOU, AND ME.
BUT YOUR FRIENDS HAVE NO PROTECTION.
IF THEY'RE WITHIN 30 MILES WHEN THE DEVICE GOES OFF...
...THEY'LL DIE--HORRIBLY.

CHANNEL'S LIVE, DOC.
TELL THEM, CHILD. TELL THEM TO FALL BACK.
HELP!! GET ME OUT OF HERE!!
SHE SAYS YOU'RE GOING TO DIIIEEE!
NOT PRECISELY WHAT I HAD IN MIND, BUT IT WILL DO.
WE'RE COMING, KID, JUST HOLD ON, WE'LL GET YOU BACK!
MS. PARKER? I THOUGHT YOU'D BEEN...PUT DOWN.
DOWN, BUT NOT OUT.
YOUNG MS. PREISS' HISTRIONICS ASIDE, SHE'S NOT WRONG ABOUT YOUR DANGER--
CHK!
CHANNEL'S DEAD.
GET US AS CLOSE AS YOU CAN. THERE'S GOT TO BE A PARACHUTE ON HERE SOMEWHERE.

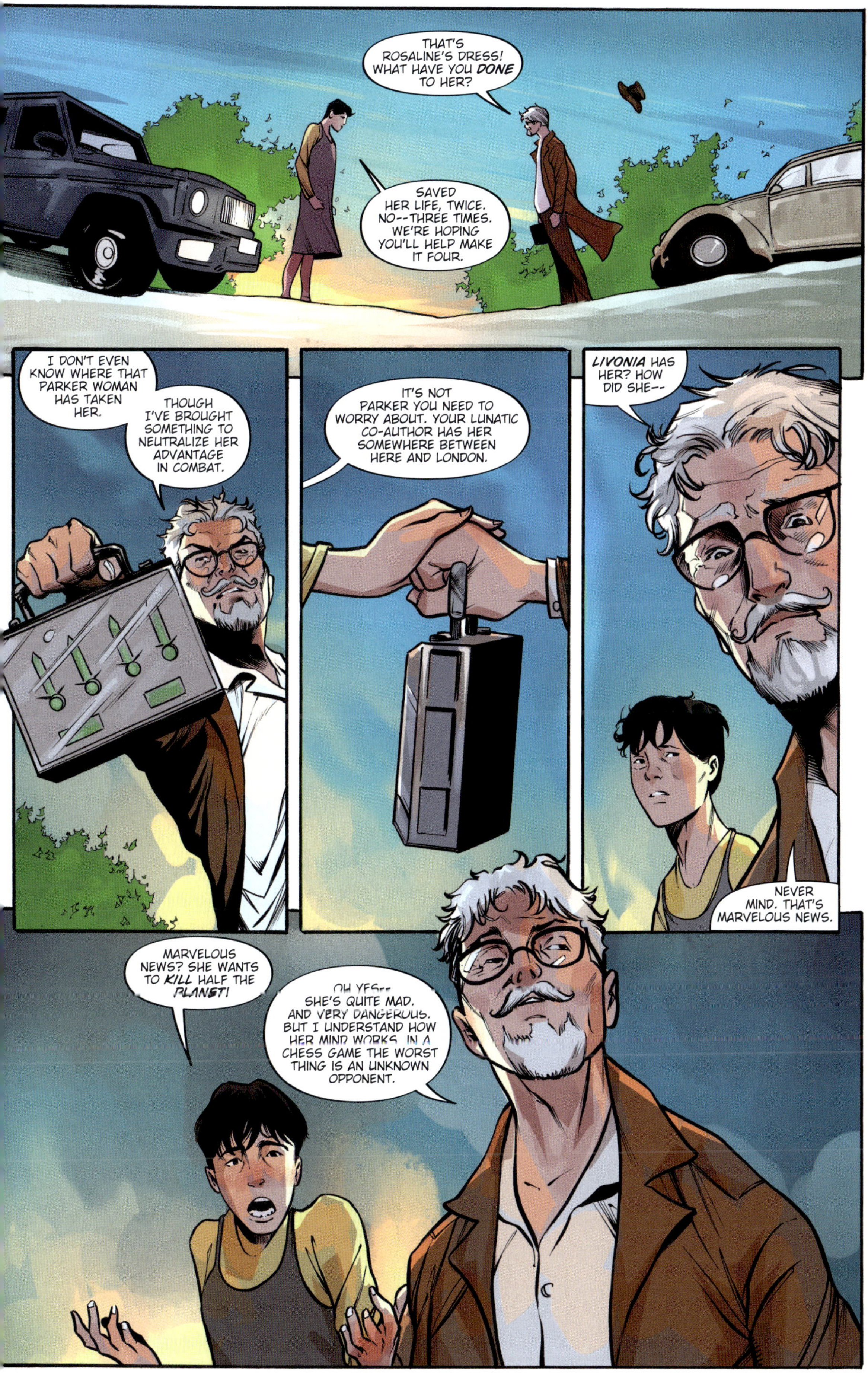
THAT'S ROSALINE'S DRESS! WHAT HAVE YOU *DONE* TO HER?
SAVED HER LIFE, TWICE. NO--THREE TIMES. WE'RE HOPING YOU'LL HELP MAKE IT FOUR.
I DON'T EVEN KNOW WHERE THAT PARKER WOMAN HAS TAKEN HER.
THOUGH I'VE BROUGHT SOMETHING TO NEUTRALIZE HER ADVANTAGE IN COMBAT.
IT'S NOT PARKER YOU NEED TO WORRY ABOUT. YOUR LUNATIC CO-AUTHOR HAS HER SOMEWHERE BETWEEN HERE AND LONDON.
LIVONIA HAS HER? HOW DID SHE--
NEVER MIND. THAT'S MARVELOUS NEWS.
MARVELOUS NEWS? SHE WANTS TO *KILL* HALF THE *PLANET!*
OH YES-- SHE'S QUITE MAD. AND VERY DANGEROUS. BUT I UNDERSTAND HOW HER MIND WORKS. IN A CHESS GAME THE WORST THING IS AN UNKNOWN OPPONENT.

"I'D THINK THE WORST THING IS AN INSANE PERSON WITH A BIOLOGICAL WEAPON, BUT LET'S AGREE TO DISAGREE."

PASSING GRAVESEND, DOC.

CARRY IT ONE KILOMETER DUE WEST, THEN BREAK THE SEAL IN THE LARGEST CROWD YOU CAN FIND.

WE'LL COLLECT YOU AT THE RENDEZVOUS POINT.

THIS STUFF WON'T HURT ME? YOU'RE SURE?

NOT ONCE THE ANTISERUM TAKES EFFECT. SHOULD ONLY TAKE A MINUTE.

"SHOULD"?

JUMP ON MY SIGNAL, MR. STECKLER.

"TELL THEM, DOCTOR."

YOU SEE, THERE'S AN ANTIBODY AND AN AGENT-- THE ANTIBODY IS PROTECTIVE, THE AGENT IS DEADLY.

SPREADS ON CONTACT, LIKE WILDFIRE, LIKE COMBUSTION. EACH DESTROYED CELL TRIGGERS THE NEXT.

YOUR TURN, MR. BRAUN. 90 MINUTES OF PROTECTION. LET'S NOT CUT THIS TOO CLOSE.
...BUT THEY'RE THE SAME CELL, THE ANTIBODY AND THE AGENT--JUST WITH REVERSED POLARITY. ONE TURNS ON THE SIGNAL, THE OTHER TURNS IT OFF. YOU UNDERSTAND?
NOT REALLY. HOW DOES THIS HELP US, CESAR?
"PROFESSOR, TELL THEM WHAT YOU DID."
I...EXCHANGED THEM. LIKE SWAPPING A PAWN FOR A QUEEN--THE WEAKEST PIECE BECOMES THE STRONGEST.
"NOW THE JACKET IS DEADLY, AND THE AGENT IS SAFE."

AAHKSSH!

BUT--WON'T CUTLER INJECT HERSELF WITH THE ANTIBODY? AND ANYONE SHE WANTS TO KEEP SAFE?
EXACTLY! DOOMED BY HER OWN HAND. POETIC JUSTICE.
"BUT THAT MIGHT INCLUDE YOUR DAUGHTER!"
OH, SHE'S ENTIRELY SAFE--I GAVE HER PERMANENT IMMUNITY. HAD TO. OTHERWISE THE EXPOSED JACKET WOULD'VE KILLED HER LONG AGO.
"SHE WON'T BE HARMED EVEN IF TRIGGERED CELLS GET ON HER. THEY CAN'T ACTIVATE HER CELLS THE WAY THEY WOULD YOURS OR MINE. SHE'S IN NO DANGER WHATSOEVER."
"NO DANGER? DAMN IT, PREISS, WHO'S FLYING THE PLANE?"
PLANE?

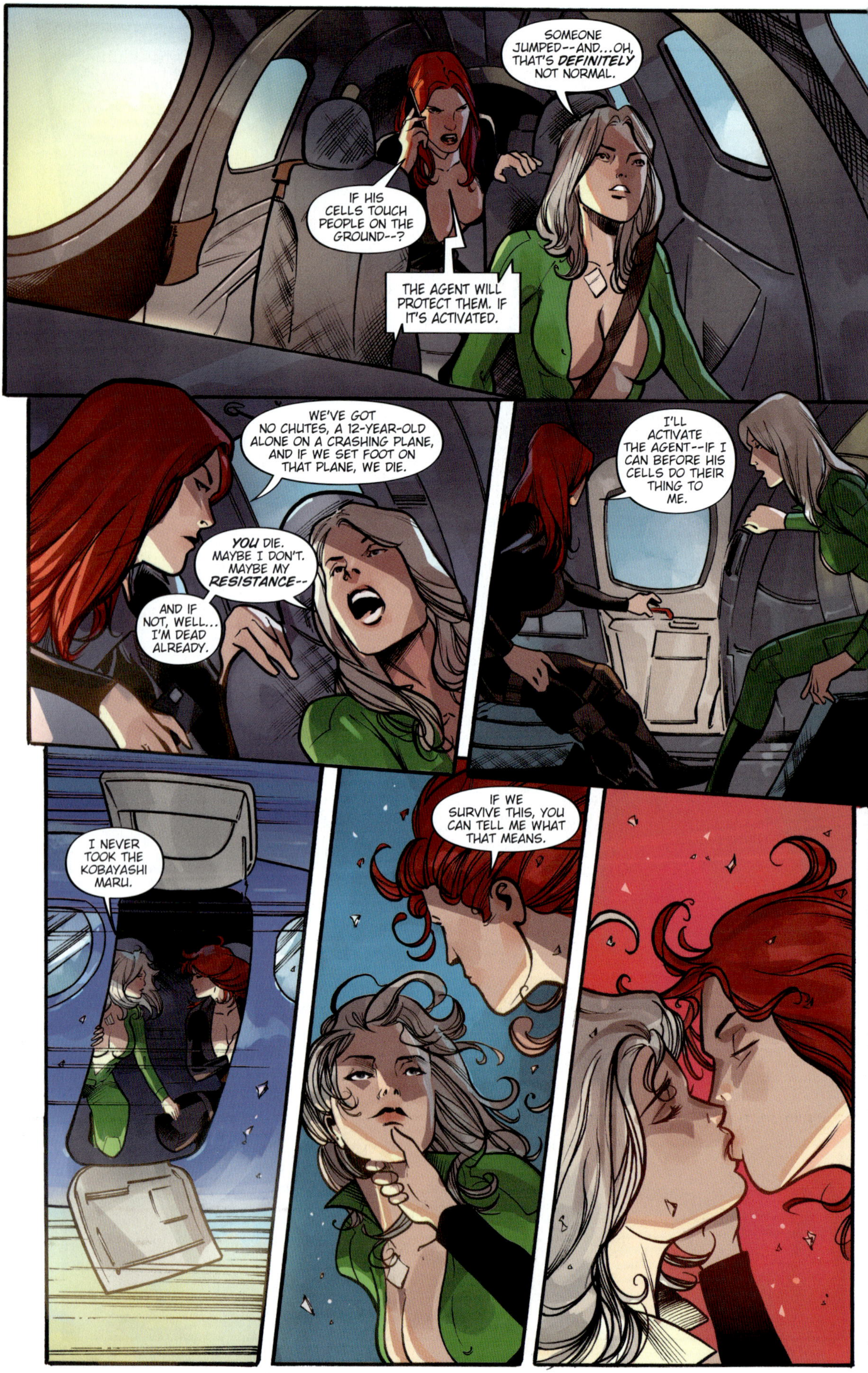

SOMEONE JUMPED--AND...OH, THAT'S DEFINITELY NOT NORMAL.
IF HIS CELLS TOUCH PEOPLE ON THE GROUND--?
THE AGENT WILL PROTECT THEM. IF IT'S ACTIVATED.
WE'VE GOT NO CHUTES, A 12-YEAR-OLD ALONE ON A CRASHING PLANE, AND IF WE SET FOOT ON THAT PLANE, WE DIE.
YOU DIE. MAYBE I DON'T. MAYBE MY RESISTANCE--
AND IF NOT, WELL... I'M DEAD ALREADY.
I'LL ACTIVATE THE AGENT--IF I CAN BEFORE HIS CELLS DO THEIR THING TO ME.
I NEVER TOOK THE KOBAYASHI MARU.
IF WE SURVIVE THIS, YOU CAN TELL ME WHAT THAT MEANS.

A DIVE FROM 30,000 FEET LASTS 150 SECONDS.

IT CAN FEEL LIKE FOREVER OR LIKE NO TIME AT ALL.

BET 30 SECONDS FELT LIKE FOREVER FOR THIS GUY.

AND I MIGHT NOT HAVE EVEN 30 SECONDS LEFT.

YANK!

FWOPPP!
COME ON. TURN DAMN IT.
GOD, I REALLY HOPE PREISS WAS RIGHT ABOUT THIS...
DON'T COME IN!
YOU'RE GOING TO DIE!
I'M GOING TO LAND THIS PLANE, IS WHAT I'M GOING TO DO.
WHAT HAPPENS AFTER THAT... THAT'S ABOVE MY PAY GRADE, KID.

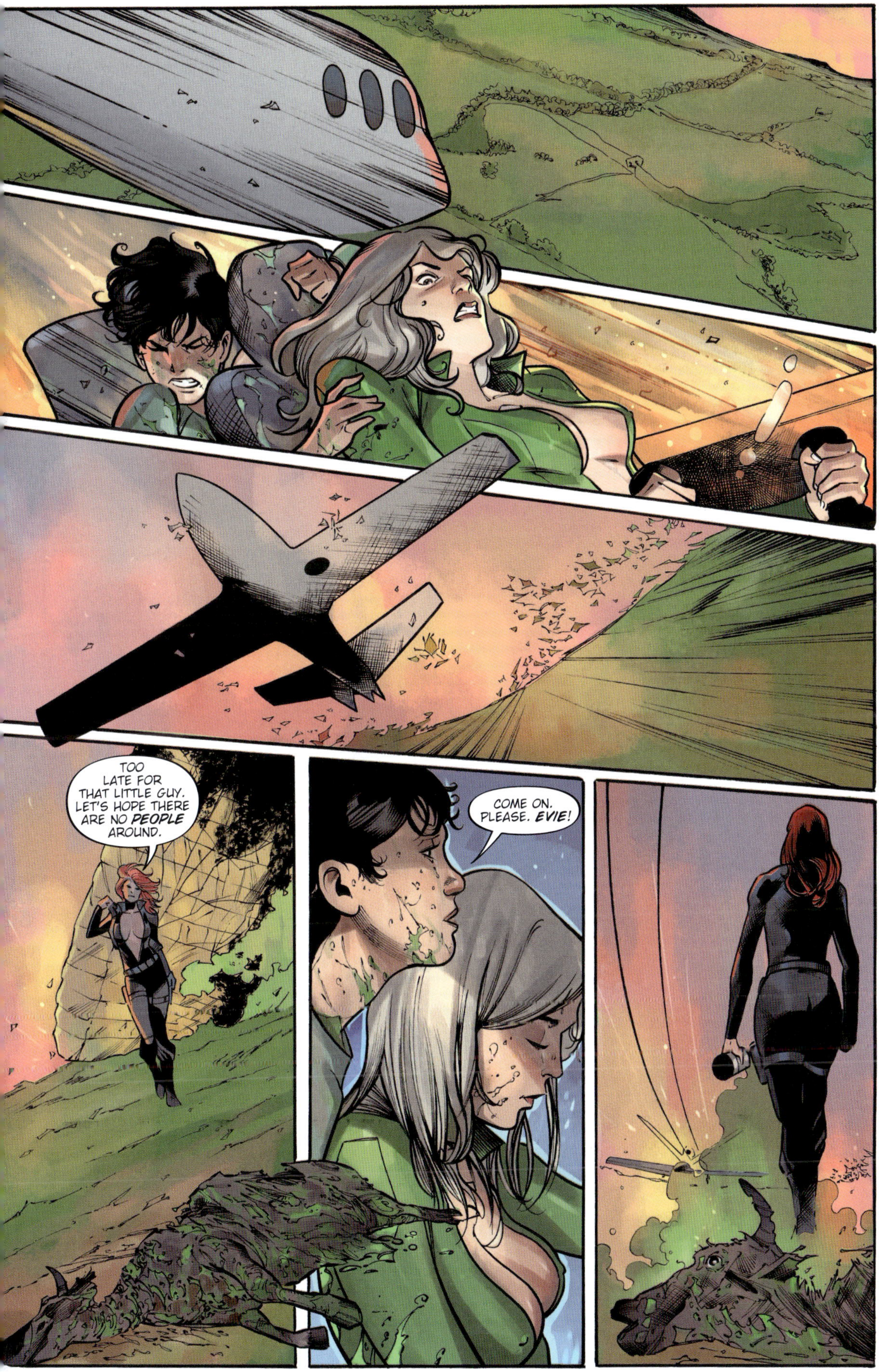
TOO LATE FOR THAT LITTLE GUY. LET'S HOPE THERE ARE NO *PEOPLE* AROUND.
COME ON. PLEASE. *EVIE!*

EVIE COLLAPSED!
COUGH--
GET HER FEET.
CAN YOU HELP HER? MAYBE THAT STUFF YOU BROUGHT?
OH NO, THAT WOULD BE THE WORST THING WE COULD DO--
THIS CHEMICAL WOULD SUPPRESS ALL HER RESISTANCES FOR THE NEXT 90 MINUTES, AND THOSE RESISTANCES ARE WHAT ARE KEEPING HER ALIVE RIGHT NOW.

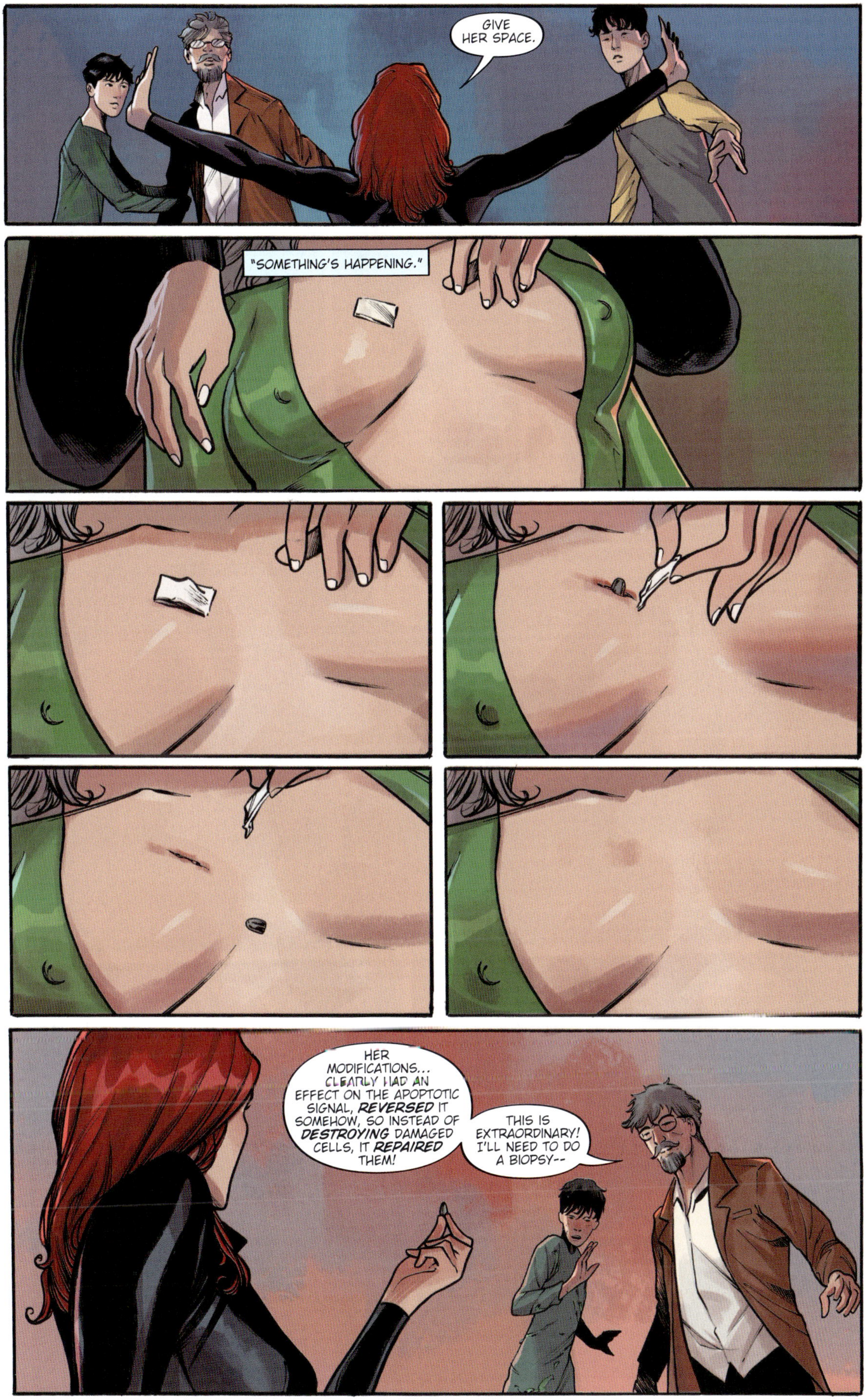
GIVE HER SPACE.
"SOMETHING'S HAPPENING."
HER MODIFICATIONS... CLEARLY HAD AN EFFECT ON THE APOPTOTIC SIGNAL, **REVERSED** IT SOMEHOW, SO INSTEAD OF **DESTROYING** DAMAGED CELLS, IT **REPAIRED** THEM!
THIS IS EXTRAORDINARY! I'LL NEED TO DO A BIOPSY--

STAY AWAY FROM HER! *YOU* DID THIS TO HER! YOU DID IT TO *ME*! YOU DID IT TO *EVERYONE*!
BUT HER BODY HAS HEALED ITSELF! AND EVERYONE'S SAFE-- THANKS TO YOU. YOU SAVED MILLIONS OF LIVES.
FROM YOU!
WHAT...WHAT HAPPENED...?
IT'S, UH--IT'S A WOLVERINE THING.
COME BACK WITH ME, WE'LL TALK, I'LL EXPLAIN--
I'LL NEVER TALK TO YOU AGAIN.
IT'S OKAY. IT'S OKAY.
YOU HIRED ME TO HELP HER DISAPPEAR. AND THAT'S WHAT I'M GOING TO DO.

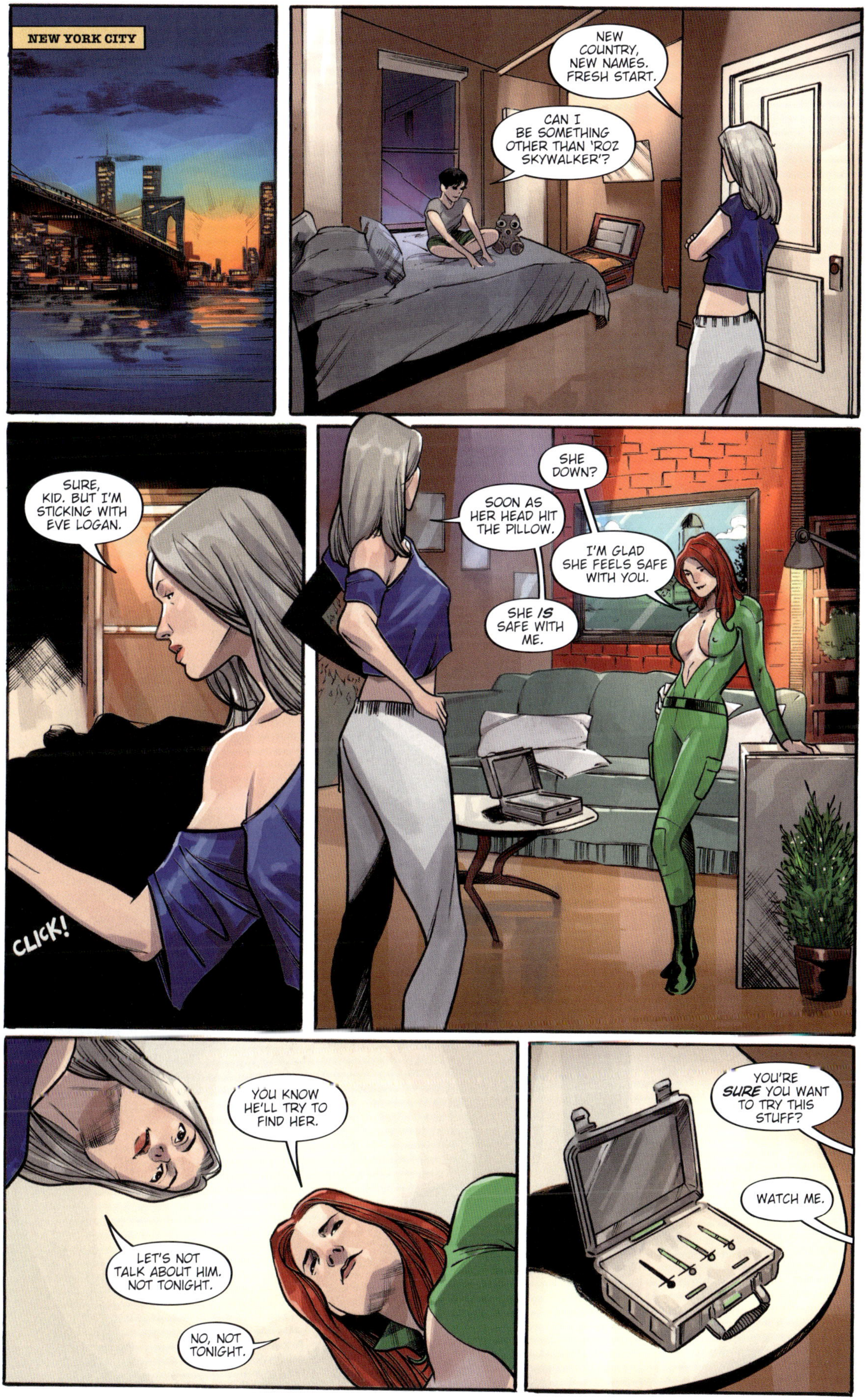
NEW YORK CITY
NEW COUNTRY, NEW NAMES. FRESH START.
CAN I BE SOMETHING OTHER THAN 'ROZ SKYWALKER'?
SURE, KID. BUT I'M STICKING WITH EVE LOGAN.
CLICK!
SHE DOWN?
SOON AS HER HEAD HIT THE PILLOW.
I'M GLAD SHE FEELS SAFE WITH YOU.
SHE *IS* SAFE WITH ME.
YOU KNOW HE'LL TRY TO FIND HER.
LET'S NOT TALK ABOUT HIM. NOT TONIGHT.
NO, NOT TONIGHT.
YOU'RE *SURE* YOU WANT TO TRY THIS STUFF?
WATCH ME.

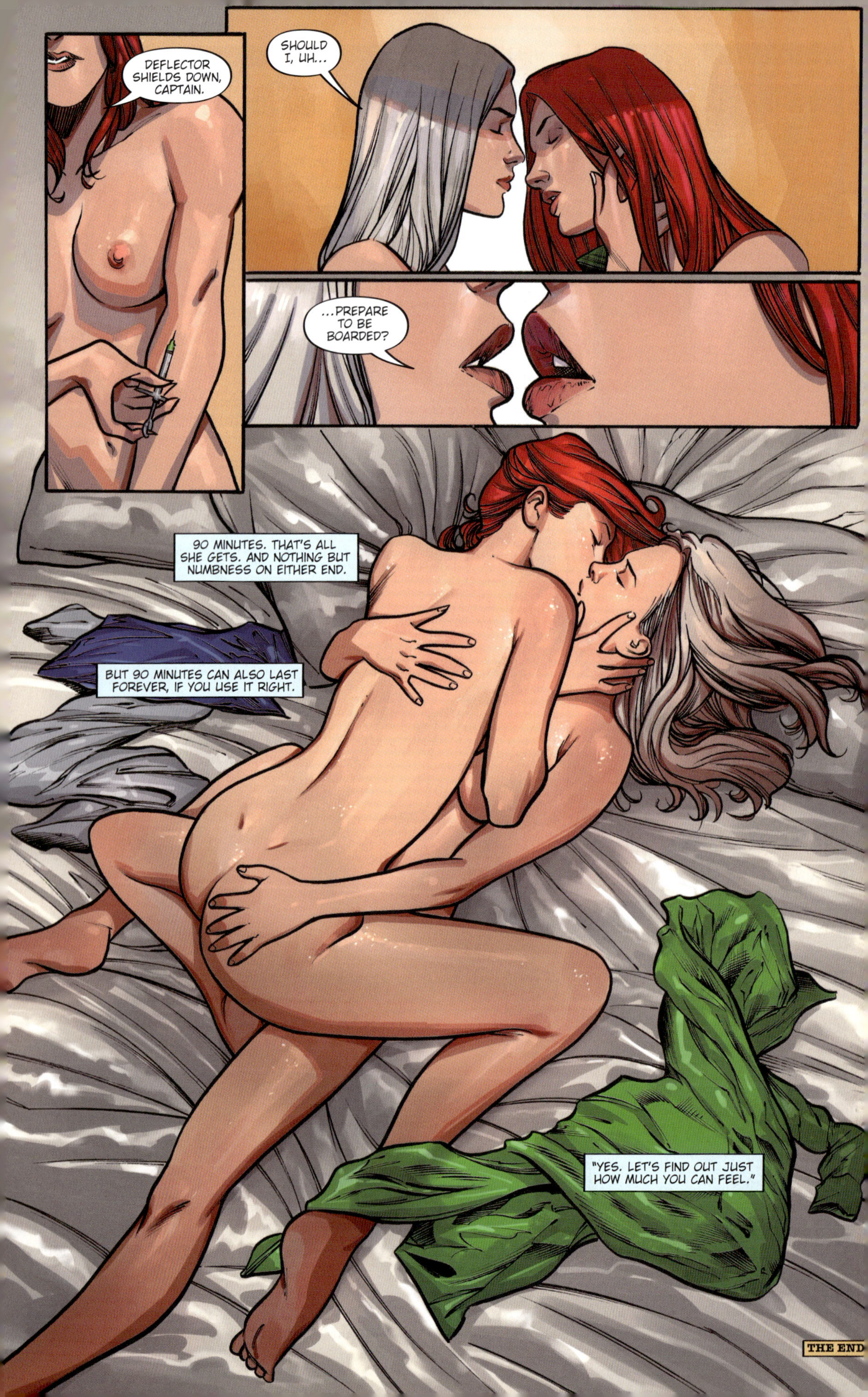
DEFLECTOR SHIELDS DOWN, CAPTAIN.
SHOULD I, UH...
...PREPARE TO BE BOARDED?
90 MINUTES. THAT'S ALL SHE GETS. AND NOTHING BUT NUMBNESS ON EITHER END.
BUT 90 MINUTES CAN ALSO LAST FOREVER, IF YOU USE IT RIGHT.
"YES. LET'S FIND OUT JUST HOW MUCH YOU CAN FEEL."
THE END

Model: Grace McClung

COVERS GALLERY

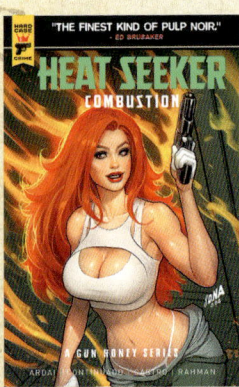

Issue #1 Cover A
David Nakayama

Issue #1 Cover B
Tula Lotay

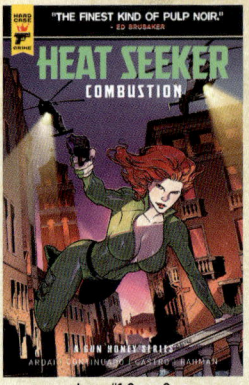

Issue #1 Cover C
Ace Continuado

Issue #1 Cover D
Model: Grace McClung @graciecosplay

Issue #1 Cover E
Lesley Li

Issue #1 Cover F
Bräo

Issue #1 Foil Cover G
David Nakayama

Issue #1 Cover H
Tula Lotay

Issue #1 Cover I
Lesley Li

Issue #1 Mix-Print Cover J
Bräo

Issue #1 INCV Cover
David Nakayama

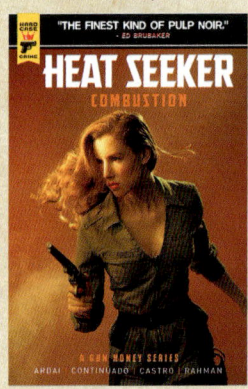

Issue #1 FOC Photo Cover - Model: Marisa Roper; Nechama Leitner/Photography

Issue #1 Pack Exclusive Cover
Model: Grace McClung @graciecosplay

Issue #1 Pack 2 Exclusive Cover - Model: Marisa Roper; Nechama Leitner/Photography

Issue #1 616 Comics
Noobovich

Issue #1 616 Comics
Noobovich

COVERS GALLERY

Issue #1 616 Comics
Cedric Poulat

Issue #1 616 Comics
Cedric Poulat

Issue #1 Stadium Comics
Nuno Pereira

Issue #1 White Dog Comics
Alain Nip

Issue #1 Davis Rider Comics
Dalmos

Issue #1 Davis Rider Comics
Dalmos

Issue #1 Davis Rider Comics
Karina Belous

Issue #1 Davis Rider Comics
Karina Belous

Issue #1 Davis Rider Comics
Karina Belous

Issue #2 Cover A
Derrick Chew

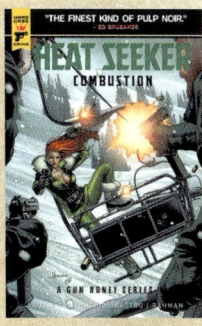

Issue #2 Cover B
Jay Anacleto & Marco Lesko

Issue #2 Cover C
Ace Continuado

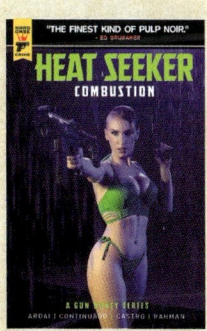

Issue #2 Cover D – Model: Grace McClung, @graciecosplay

Issue #2 Cover E
Thaddeus Robeck

Issue #2 Cover F
Thaddeus Robeck

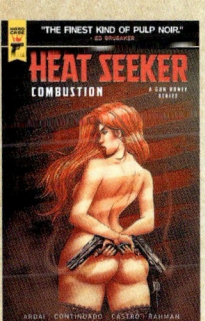

Issue #2 Cover G
Bräo

Issue #2 Cover H Virgin Foil
Derrick Chew

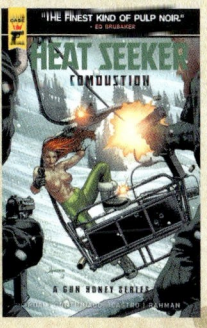

Issue #2 Cover I
Jay Anacleto & Marco Lesko

Issue #2 INCV Cover
Derrick Chew

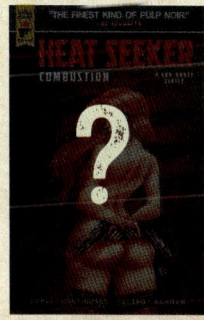

Issue #2 Mix-Print Cover K
Bräo

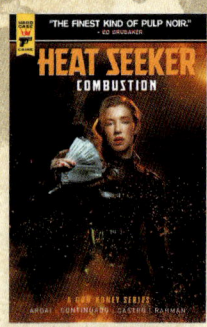

Issue #2 FOC Photo Cover. Model: Marisa Roper, Nechama Leitner/Photography

Issue #2 616 Comics
Kyuyong Eom

Issue #2 616 Comics
Kyuyong Eom

Issue #2 616 Comics
Cedric Poulat

Issue #2 616 Comics
Cedric Poulat

Issue #2 White Dog Comics
Tiago da Silva

Issue #2 White Dog Comics
Derrick Chew

Issue #2 White Dog Comics
Miki Okazaki

Issue #3 Cover A
Kendrick Lim

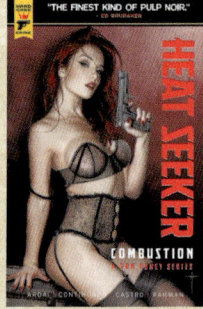

Issue #3 Cover B
Jay Ferguson

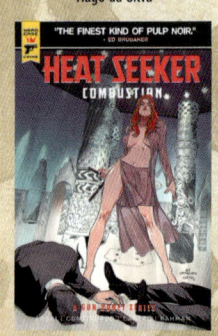

Issue #3 Cover C
Ace Continuado

Issue #3 Cover D – Model: Grace McClung, @graciecosplay

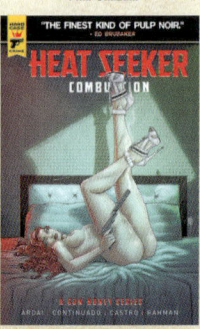

Issue #3 Cover E
Brão

Issue #3 Foil Cover
Kendrick Lim

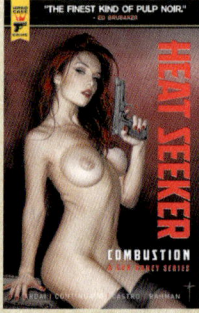

Issue #3 Cover G
Jay Ferguson

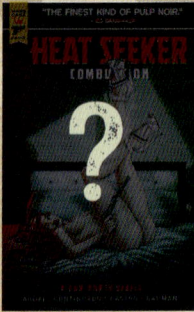

Issue #3 Mix-Print Cover H
Brão

Issue #3 Cover I
Kendrick Lim

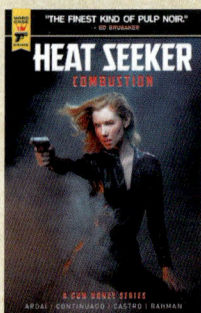

Issue #3 Cover J – Model: Marisa Roper, Nechama Leitner/Photography

Issue #3 616 Comics
Ivan Talavera

Issue #3 616 Comics
Ivan Talavera

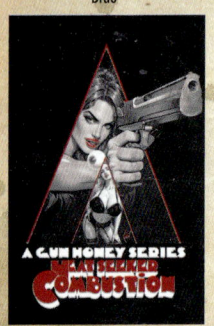

Issue #3 616 Comics
Cedric Poulat

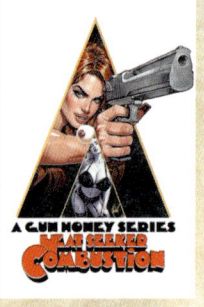

Issue #3 616 Comics
Cedric Poulat

Issue #3 White Dog Comics
Tiago da Silva

Issue #3 Blank Cover Podcast
Marco Turini

Issue #3 Comic Kingdom
John Gallagher

Issue #3 Comic Kingdom
John Gallagher

Issue #3 Comic Kingdom
John Gallagher

Issue #4 Cover A
Ivan Tao

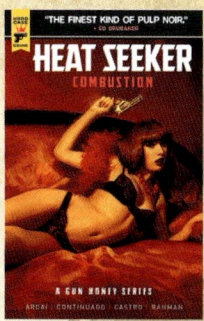

Issue #4 Cover B
Irvin Rodriguez

Issue #4 Cover C
Ace Continuado

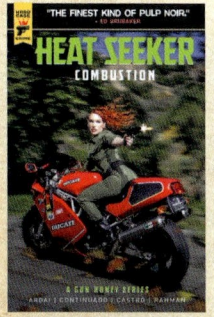

Issue #4 Cover D – Model: Grace
McClung, @graciecosplay

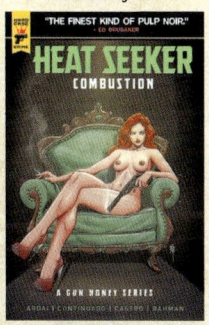

Issue #4 Cover E
Bräo

Issue #4 Cover F
Ivan Tao

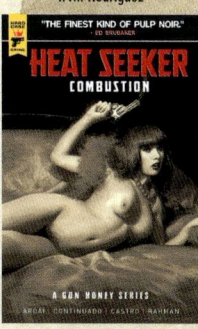

Issue #4 Cover G
Irvin Rodriguez

Issue #4 Mix-Print Cover H
Bräo

Issue #4 Cover I
Ivan Tao

Issue #4 Cover J – Model: Marisa
Roper, Photo: Shea Gordon

Issue #4 616 Comics
Cedric Poulat

Issue #4 616 Comics
Cedric Poulat

Issue #4 616 Comics
Jay Ferguson

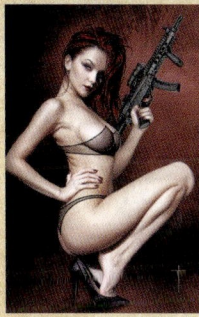

Issue #4 616 Comics
Jay Ferguson

Issue #4 Tuxedo Tiger Comics
Dalmos

Issue #4 Tuxedo Tiger Comics
Dalmos

Issue #4 White Dog Comics
Ivan Tao

Issue #4 White Dog Comics
Ivan Tao

Issue #4 White Dog Comics
Shyguyz

Issue #4 White Dog Comics
Shyguyz

Issue #4 White Dog Comics
Tiago da Silva

Issue #4 White Dog Comics
Tiago da Silva

MY SUPER EX-GIRLFRIEND

BY **JOANNA TAN**, AKA GUN HONEY

So you want to know about Dahlia Racers. Where do I start?

Yes, we dated. It didn't last, but not for the reasons you might think. When we met, I was still new to the U.S., making a name for myself in the weapons business. Dahlia was helping a man disappear, a little fish who'd turned state's evidence to put a bigger fish behind bars. He was in the international heroin trade, and those people take their betrayals seriously. No amount of Witness Protection would protect him.

Dahlia offered me ten thousand dollars to switch guns on the man hired to kill him, and another ten to switch them back after. It wasn't worth risking my life even once for that money, never mind twice -- but there's something about Dahlia that makes you want to say yes. She'd say it's her charisma. I think it's more her reckless disregard for her own safety. It's clear she's going ahead with or without you, and you don't want to see this beautiful, eager, smart, talented woman wind up in pieces in the water off Breezy Point. Not when she's asking for your help and you can give it.

I told her to keep her money, I'd do it for a dinner at Rao's, if she could use that charisma of hers to get us a table. I watched her make two phone calls. She lied her ass off both times, and damned if we didn't get the table. It was a good preview of what life with her would be like.

Fast forward from commiserating over negronis about the men we worked for to breakfast at her place and no more talk of men at all. A month later we had a place in the Flatiron District and knew who liked the toilet paper rolled under and who liked it over. (Me, her.) Also, easily the best sex I've ever had. The woman's a fucking wizard with her tongue.

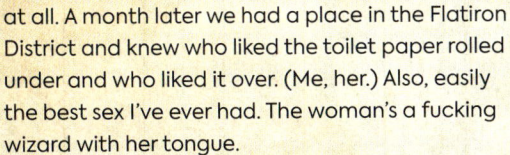

So what broke us up? Was it her other women? No. It's only cheating if either of you minds, and I didn't. Were we competitive about work? Hardly. She does things I could never do, and I know she'd say the same.

It was just... centrifugal force. I was getting more jobs on the West Coast, more work in Asia; she's a New York girl, and was working a lot in Europe. We just found ourselves in separate worlds, home less, apart for months at a time.

But damn. There's no one I'd sooner trust with my life -- I *did* trust her with it, last year, when those government agents were trying to kill me, and I'd do it again. You certainly can, if that's what you want to know.

Ah, you do know? Good -- then it's just a question of whether she'll break your heart. And you know what? Maybe. They call her Heat Seeker for a reason, and you'll never keep her from chasing the hottest flame. But it'll be worth it.

So wait, tell me again -- how did the two of you meet...?

THE DIVINE MISS M

Not just anyone can play one of the leading ladies in the GUN HONEY universe. Take Dahlia Racers, for instance. Filling the jumpsuit of this ingenious, resourceful action hero calls for more than just beauty. You need charisma, presence, star quality, stamina -- and it helps to know how to fight.

Enter Marisa Roper, New York-based actress, model, singer, screenwriter, triathlete, and marathon runner, currently studying kung fu and Mandarin at Yunnan Temple in China.

One of the international circuit's most in-demand models, her work can be seen everywhere from *Vogue* to NYFW to commercials for brands such as Nikon, Olympus, and Sony. Also an accomplished actress, she has performed off-Broadway, around the country, and on screens from Bollywood (*Election War* starring Rituparna Sengupta) to Amazon Prime (*Two Cents from a Pariah*; next year's *Post Truth* and *Privateers*).

Always a lover of words, she tied for first place in the O. Henry World Pun Championships in 2018 with a 90-second-long pun performance. She founded her production company Apple Butta Productions in 2021, and has since produced original narrative films and documentaries in New York, Maryland, and New Orleans.

Marisa is one of the brightest rising stars we know, and when we discovered she happens to also have a passion for crime stories and comics and loved the idea of embodying our crimson-maned femme fatale, we couldn't miss the chance to have her grace our covers.

When, inevitably, you see her starring in some future *Avengers* battle royal on the silver screen, just remember – you saw her here first.

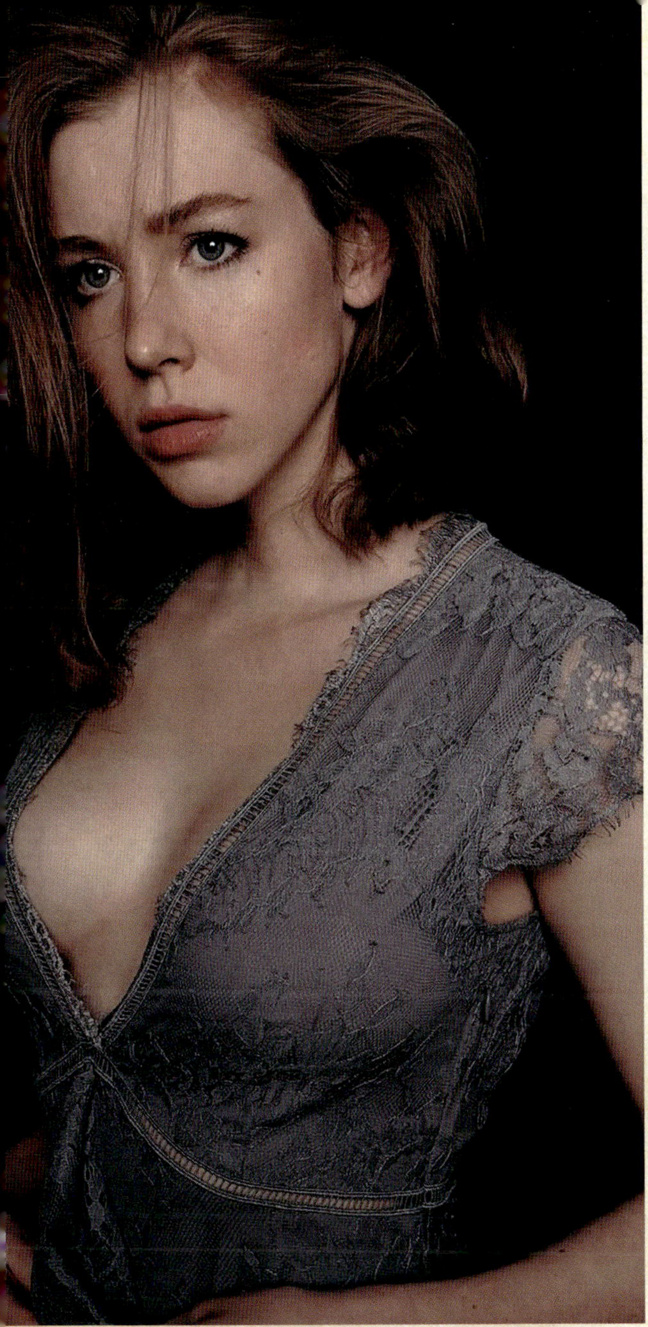
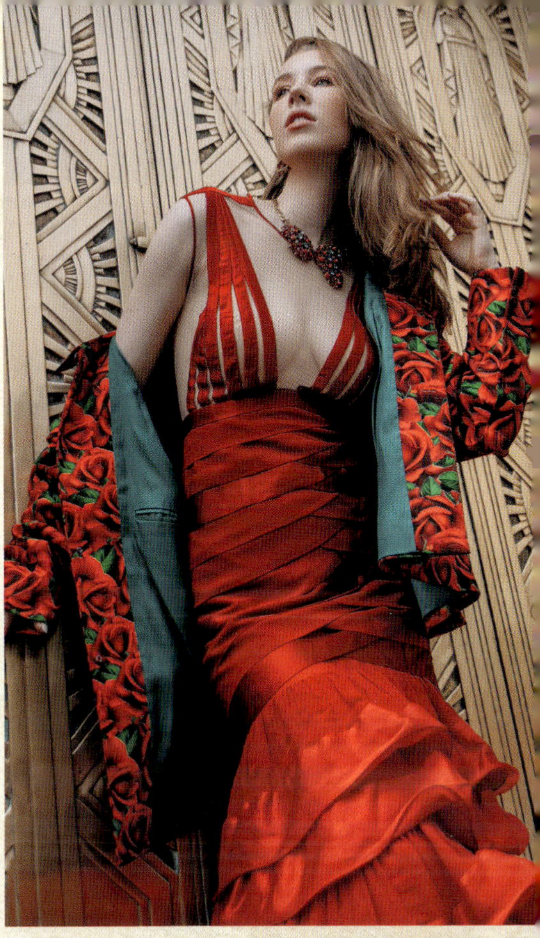
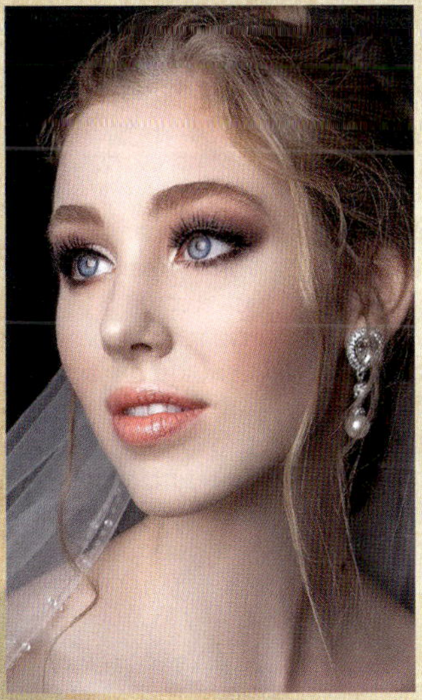
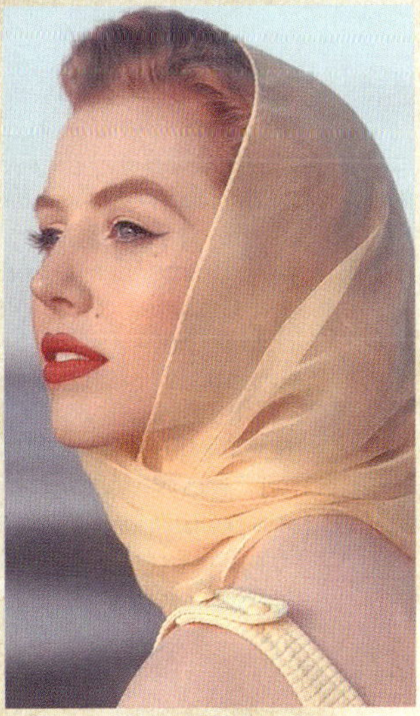
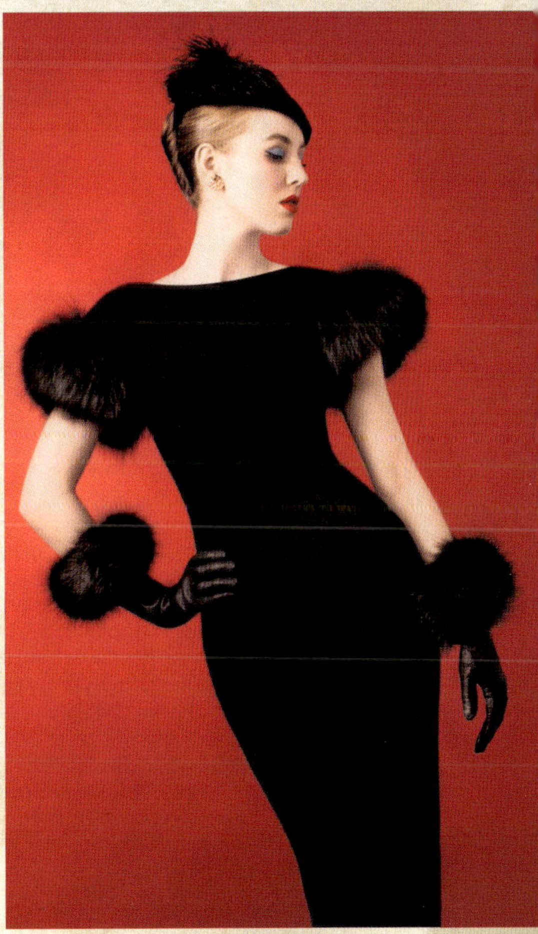

EXTRA, EXTRA! READ ALL ABOUT IT!

Back in the day, any issue of a comic book had just a single cover. If you wanted to see another cover, you waited a month for the next issue. That's just the way it was.

But at some point some wise soul had the insight that it didn't need to be that way -- multiple artists could get a crack at illustrating the cover of a given issue, offering multiple visions of what that issue could look like and giving fans a range of variants (some common, some rare) to add to their collections.

We love variant covers. Especially when your storylines only run four issues long, as ours do, variants give you the opportunity to work with dozens of amazing artists rather than only a few (and with more cosplay models too), giving chances to some newcomers that -- who knows? -- might be superstars tomorrow.

One result of commissioning all these extra cover images, though, is that we've sometimes ended up with more variants than we've been able to publish. We thought it would be fun to give you a look here at some of the pieces we haven't gotten to use. Julia Puche Pérez from Spain, for instance, whose work recalls classic movie posters from the 1950s and 60s, painted Dahlia outdoors in a snowstorm. Thad Robeck's cover for the first HEAT SEEKER series had an outdoor variant as well, with a gorgeous sunset overhead.

Ace Continuado drew his sauna cover for Issue 3 in clothed and nude versions, but in the end we only wound up using the former on a cover — you can see the more NSFW version here. Meanwhile, Irvin Rodriguez's nude variant for Issue 4 of the current series is getting printed only in a cool black-and-white version; this is your chance to see it in full color. And photo-cover models Grace McClung and Marisa Roper are each represented by a photo we loved but just ran out of slots to run.

Our thanks to all these talented artists for their amazing work. We'll keep bringing you as much of it as we can. And when, occasionally, our cup runneth over...watch these back pages for cool extras!

ACE EXPOSED!

As Dahlia Racers' second adventure draws to a close, we want to give a tip of the hat to the brilliant artist who draws her: Ace Continuado. Originally from the Philippines (where he worked as a dentist – a first profession he shares with gunslinger Doc Holliday, novelist Zane Grey, and Revolutionary War hero Paul Revere – and as a drummer in rock and heavy metal bands), Ace made his comic book debut in 2013 on *Super Action Man* for 215 Ink. Since then, he's drawn for Dark Horse, Zenoscope, Titan, Counterpoint, Advent and more, lending his stylish and dynamic line to books such as *Shaper*, *Red Agent*, *Robyn Hood*, and of course...*Heat Seeker*.

Watching a page of Ace's art unfold, with its dramatic angles, gorgeous settings, and lithe figures bursting past his panels' borders, feels like sitting in a darkened theater watching a great action movie unspool.

Now living in California with wife Maria, daughter Camila, and their beloved cats, Ace is already hard at work on Dahlia's return: look for

HEAT SEEKER EXPOSED to debut in May 2025. How much more exposed could Dahlia get, you might wonder? Well, with an investigative reporter on her trail and all her clients' secrets at stake, Dahlia has a new and deadlier sort of exposure to worry about.

As for Ace? He's earned every bit of exposure that HEAT SEEKER is giving him, and we trust it'll lead to nothing but great things — hopefully including plenty more death-defying adventures for our favorite diva of deception...

FROM TITAN COMICS AND HARD CASE CRIME

GRAPHIC NOVELS

THE ASSIGNMENT
BABYLON BERLIN
THE BIG HOAX
BREAKNECK
FRANK LEE: AFTER ALCATRAZ
GAMMA DRACONIS
GUN HONEY VOLUMES 1-3
HEAT SEEKER: A GUN HONEY SERIES VOLUME 1
MILLENNIUM: THE GIRL WITH THE DRAGON TATTOO
MILLENNIUM: THE GIRL WHO PLAYED WITH FIRE
MILLENNIUM: THE GIRL WHO KICKED THE HORNET'S NEST
MILLENNIUM: THE GIRL WHO DANCED WITH DEATH
MINKY WOODCOCK: THE GIRL WHO HANDCUFFED HOUDINI
MINKY WOODCOCK: THE GIRL WHO ELECTRIFIED TESLA
MINKY WOODCOCK: THE GIRL CALLED CTHULHU
MICKEY SPILLANE'S MIKE HAMMER

MS. TREE: ONE MEAN MOTHER
MS. TREE: SKELETON IN THE CLOSET
MS. TREE: THE COLD DISH
MS. TREE: DEADLINE
MS. TREE: HEROINE WITHDRAWAL
MS TREE: FALLEN TREE
NOIR BURLESQUE
NORMANDY GOLD
PEEPLAND
THE PRAGUE COUP
QUARRY'S WAR
RYUKO VOLUMES 1 & 2
TRIGGERMAN
TYLER CROSS: BLACK ROCK
TYLER CROSS: ANGOLA
WILL EISNER'S JOHN LAW

NOVELS

361
THE ACTOR (AKA MEMORY)
ARE SNAKES NECESSARY?
THE BIG BUNDLE
BLACKMAILER
BLOOD ON THE MINK
BLOOD SUGAR
A BLOODY BUSINESS
BORDERLINE
BRAINQUAKE
BROTHERS KEEPERS
BUST
CALL ME A CAB
CASTLE IN THE AIR
CHARLESGATE CONFIDENTIAL
CHOKE HOLD
THE COCKTAIL WAITRESS
THE COLORADO KID
THE COMEDY IS FINISHED
THE CONSUMMATA
THE COUNT OF 9
CUT ME IN
THE CUTIE
DEAD STREET
DEADLY BELOVED
DEATH COMES TOO LATE
A DIET OF TREACLE
DOUBLE DOWN
DOUBLE FEATURE
EASY DEATH
FADE TO BLONDE
FAST CHARLIE
FIFTY-TO-ONE
FIVE DECEMBERS
FOOLS DIE ON FRIDAY
FOREVER AND A DEATH

THE GET OFF
GETTING OFF: A NOVEL OF SEX AND VIOLENCE
THE GIRL WITH THE DEEP BLUE EYES
THE GIRL WITH THE LONG GREEN HEART
GRIFTER'S GAME
GUN WORK
THE GUTTER AND THE GRAVE
HELP I AM BEING HELD PRISONER
HONEY IN HIS MOUTH
THE HOT BEAT
HOW LIKE A GOD
INTO THE NIGHT
JOYLAND
KILLER, COME BACK TO ME
KILLING CASTRO
THE KNIFE SLIPPED
THE LAST STAND
LATER
LEMONS NEVER LIE
LITTLE GIRL LOST
LOWDOWN ROAD
LUCKY AT CARDS
MAD MONEY
THE MAX
MONEY SHOT
THE NEXT TIME I DIE
THE NICE GUYS
NIGHT WALKER
NOBODY'S ANGEL
NO HOUSE LIMIT
PIMP
ROBBIE'S WIFE
THE SECRET LIVES OF MARRIED WOMEN
SEED ON THE WIND
SHILLS CAN'T CASH CHIPS
SINNER MAN

SKIM DEEP
SLIDE
SNATCH
SO MANY DOORS
SO NUDE, SO DEAD
SOHO SINS
SOMEBODY OWES ME MONEY
SONGS OF INNOCENCE
THIEVES FALL OUT
TOO MANY BULLETS
TOP OF THE HEAP
TOUGH TENDER
THE TRIUMPH OF THE SPIDER MONKEY
TURN ON THE HEAT
THE TWENTY-YEAR DEATH
TWO FOR THE MONEY
UNDERSTUDY FOR DEATH
THE VALLEY OF FEAR
THE VENGEFUL VIRGIN

QUARRY

THE FIRST QUARRY
KILLING QUARRY
THE LAST QUARRY
QUARRY
QUARRY'S BLOOD
QUARRY'S CHOICE
QUARRY'S CLIMAX
QUARRY'S CUT
QUARRY'S DEAL
QUARRY'S EX
QUARRY'S LIST
QUARRY'S RETURN
QUARRY'S VOTE
QUARRY IN THE BLACK
QUARRY IN THE MIDDLE
THE WRONG QUARRY